# "So pretty, ...
## he said almost reverently

Jim bent one knee to kneel before her, putting the glass down on the deep carpeting. Neither noticed that the glass had fallen over as his hands rested on the arms of the chair and he leaned even closer to her, as though time had stopped and they had an eternity to linger over the kiss that was softly shared.

"Faith, don't condemn me now. Give me a chance," he whispered when his lips finally left hers and he had buried his head in the softness of her shoulder. "I won't change who I am, but I will please you. I will, if you let me."

## ABOUT THE AUTHOR

Rebecca Bond holds an M.B.A. in marketing
and has worked as an advertising copywriter
as well as an advertising account executive.
Her passion is traveling, which she feels
helps her in her writing; she has been all
over the world, including China and Japan.
A native Californian, Rebecca lives in
South San Francisco with her husband, a
federal prosecutor.

# In Passion's Defense

## REBECCA BOND

## *Harlequin Books*

TORONTO • NEW YORK • LONDON
AMSTERDAM • PARIS • SYDNEY • HAMBURG
STOCKHOLM • ATHENS • TOKYO • MILAN

Published February 1985

First printing December 1984

ISBN 0-373-16092-5

Printed in Canada

# Chapter One

Faith Karell drew the warm sheets over her shoulder and buried her head deeper into the two soft down pillows, vainly attempting to shut out the annoying persistent ringing that filled the room. Finally willing herself to move, she rolled over in the huge bed, her hand groping for the offending telephone. After knocking the receiver onto the bedside table, she lay momentarily inert, her arm dangling over the side of the bed. Then with a sigh she shook her disheveled hair out of her eyes and brought the receiver groggily to her ear, her eyes still tightly shut against the already-bright sunlight reflected from the white sands of Venice City Beach through her window.

"Hello?" Her voice was low and throaty, still filled with the last vestiges of sleep.

"Faith? Faith, are you there? Are you all right?" Her mother's tittering, birdlike voice came over the wire.

"What time is it?" She was awake now, rolling over on her back, throwing her arm over her eyes as she listened to her mother's frantic questions.

"Time for you to be up," the retort came swiftly. "But are you all right? I thought I heard banging when you answered the phone."

"I'm fine, mom. I just dropped the phone," Faith explained patiently, unable to restrain the sigh that escaped her lips.

"Now, don't sound like that." Her mother's reprimand was quick and curt. "You know how I worry about you, practicing law as you do, trying to put all those criminals away. Who knows when one of them is going to come for you after he gets out of jail?"

"Mother! I've told you a hundred times they don't get mad at me for their sentence. If their lawyers blow the case, they go after them. No one would touch an Assistant U.S. Attorney. Every cop in the country would be after him!" Even after all these years of Faith's practicing criminal law, her mother still thought of her as more like Serpico than Perry Mason.

Faith couldn't really blame her. After all, criminal law was as foreign to her as shopping at a Pack and Save grocery store. All those years of hearing her husband talk about the law in terms of million-dollar settlements rather than life sentences had colored her thinking. And her mother had never really been one to consider criminal law as a fitting career for a woman, much less her daughter. The woman was from the old school. A lady was only a lady if she was married with four children. Women who worked were just beyond her realm.

"Well, what would I do if I didn't worry about you?" her mother responded, making no sense whatsoever. The woman was so busy traveling with Faith's father or volunteering her time to her various charities that she only had time to worry about her daughters when she felt the need to play a part in their lives.

"I don't know, mom," Faith replied, humoring her. Her mother was a beautiful woman, even at the age of sixty-five, but once she opened her mouth and all her energy poured forth, the only adjective that could describe her was cute.

"Mom," Faith went on before the older woman could start in again, "what do you want?" Her eyes strayed to the clock, and her loving impatience grew as she noted that it was only six o'clock. She still had another half hour before her alarm would go off.

"Well, dear, I just wanted to tell you that you forgot to take that lovely little petit-point footstool with you when you were here for dinner last night." Faith buried her head in her pillows as she listened to her mother talk.

She hadn't forgotten the footstool; she had simply gracefully ignored it sitting beside the door as she walked out of her parents' plush home. She knew her mother meant well, but Faith's little beach house was beginning to look like the Palace at Versailles. Faith would really prefer to buy her own furniture, but Helen Karell kept insisting that she take everything in the house so that she would have an excuse to redecorate, for one thing. And besides, she hated the thought of her eldest daughter living so frugally. It simply was not done in their circles.

What her mother failed to realize was that Faith didn't run in circles even close to those she grew up in. It was her sister, Beth, who had inherited the need to live with the beautiful people, dress as though she owned Rodeo Drive, and spend as if she were the Bank of Switzerland.

"Oh, I'm sorry. I'll get it next time I'm down. But really, mom, I don't need any more furniture. You've been so generous as it is." She hoped her mother would take the gentle hint, but as usual she ignored it or didn't get it.

"Don't be silly. You can never have too much *good* furniture." The emphasis was her way of gently reprimanding Faith for living at the beach and driving a car that had to be hidden when she went to visit her parents. "Besides, just think, someday you'll be married and you'll want to make a nice home for your husband. Then you'll thank me for all the things I saved for you."

"I know I will, mom, but I think that day is a while off. Besides, one more stick of furniture and there won't be enough room in this place for a husband."

"Well, of course, you wouldn't live in Venice. My goodness, I'd expect any man you would marry to whisk you right off to Hancock Park or some such place. Southern California has so many wonderful places to live! The beach—what a silly thought." Her mother tittered into the phone, sincerely amused by her daughter's train of thought.

"Of course, mom." Faith knew when it was time to quit objecting to her mother's insistent desire that her daughter would eventually live the same life she had. Helen wanted so much for them to have something in common. Little did she know that they already had a lot in common—their mutual love.

"You know, Faith, Jim Greenly was over the other night and was asking about you." Helen could change direction faster than a trout in a stream. "He told us again that he always had a place for you in his firm. It would be so nice if you went to work there. It's such a lovely building right there in the U.C.B. high-rise, with so many nice looking young men around. He said you should call him anytime you wanted...."

"Mother, please. We've been over this a hundred times before. I like what I do and I love how I live. I really don't think I'll be calling Jim in the near future." Faith gently but finally put an end to the discussion. For once she would love it if her mother called just to say hello like other parents, but she knew that would be asking a lot.

She had never been able to make her mother understand that she felt a moral obligation to prosecute rather than defend criminals. Her father understood. Thought it was crazy that she didn't want to "go for the gold," as he would say. But nonetheless, he had admitted that there were some lawyers who simply couldn't resist the lure of government law. It was an exciting field, full of seamy characters and hard evidence. His little girl wanted to deal in absolutes: the good guys versus the bad guys. Strange that a girl who had grown up with every advantage had felt so strongly about choosing a route that would never lead to big dollars and social notoriety. Faith reminded him of his mother: a woman who could stand up to anything, live on practically nothing and still be happy. He also had to admit that he was proud of her. If only Helen could understand.

"Well, all right, dear," Helen Karell said as Faith began to bless the powers that had given her mother a short attention span. But she was immediately disappointed, as her mother proved to be on one of her crusades. "It just seems a shame that after all that hard work you went to you'll never really amount to anything. Oh, dear, I didn't mean that." Immediately flustered, her mother made small apologetic noises into the phone, and Faith giggled. When Helen Karell was embarrassed by one of her many slips of the tongue, she sounded like a tape recorder gone haywire.

"Mom, it's okay. Just try to remember that in order to amount to anything, you don't need to have a husband or a lot of money."

"Oh, yes, dear, I know that. Well, if you want that footstool, you'll let me know, won't you?" Her mother was now anxious to terminate the conversation, and Faith gladly obliged.

"I will, mom. Give my love to daddy. Bye-bye." Rolling over once more, she replaced the receiver and lay back for a few moments waiting for sleep to come once again. But rest was as elusive as a hummingbird as Faith burrowed deeper into the sheets.

A smile played about her lips as she considered what her mother had said. The message never changed. Be a little more like me, her mother seemed to be saying, not so much like your father. Too much drive isn't healthy for a woman. You'll never be married if you continue to act like a man. But Faith had to admit that even after all these years her mother's reminders that she was unmarried and likely to remain so if she continued on her present course bothered her a little.

If her mother only knew. There was nothing Faith would have liked more than to find a man she could love. A man who would understand that she wanted to do more with her life than simply have enough money to travel and buy beautiful things.

But no one ever seemed to have just the right combination of humor and strength. Perhaps it had been all those years of law school, the apprenticeship as a clerk for a federal judge, the final rigorous test of becoming an Assistant U.S. Attorney and having to prove herself as a trial lawyer. All those years had somehow passed, leaving Faith behind. Faith, who was confident as a lawyer but unsure of herself as a woman. If only her mother knew that sometimes she hated the drive within her that seemed to cause the scales of justice to rest on her shoulders alone. Where on earth had she inherited such a need to prove herself, such a desire to make a mark outside the realm of her family's fortune?

As sometimes happened, the phone call had only planted a seed that now blossomed into full-fledged anxiety. As Faith lay snuggled deep in the bed alone, the doubts again plagued her, as they did when she was so often reminded that she was different from other women. A chorus of muted sounds assaulted her ears, adding fuel to her anxiety. The beach was coming alive outside her small house. Dogs yelped, released for their morning run by owners who shuffled, yawning, down the boardwalk, oblivious of their

happy pets. Young surfers congregated on the cool
sand after their 5:00 A.M. frolic in the waves. Occasion-
ally Faith could hear the whirr of wheels as someone
on roller skates whizzed by her window.

Her mind's eye traced every inch of the beach outside her abode, which nestled unobtrusively among
the new luxury condominiums that lined the most expensive piece of real estate west of Century City.

There would be young girls and boys, their long,
streaked-blond hair falling to their shoulders in wet
ropes, standing by their surfboards now. Happy, carefree faces, tanned and creaseless, would be turned toward the early-morning sun for a minute more before
they made their way to school. They were sun flowers, blossoming as the warming rays caressed their
scantily clad bodies. They would wilt as they donned
jeans and work shirts, anticipating the classroom
hours.

The dog walkers would be older, night people,
those who made their living tending bar or waiting
tables. Some were pilots and flight attendants, but all
were aging nymphs who still lived for the sun and the
mating game that must always be played when mature
and lonesome bodies lay oiled on the steaming sand.
They were the beautiful, aging wanderers who inhab-
ited the California beaches, coming from all over the
United States, chasing one more moment of youth.

And all of them knew only the thrill of the physical.
Each was possessed with a body toned to perfection by
bicycle riding or roller skating. Here at the beach, it
was the kiss of social death to ignore the physical.
Chests and legs, arms and waists, were gorgeous

masses of glittering muscle shown to their best advantage, covered with only the shortest shorts and the smallest, tightest tank tops.

Then there was Faith, a stranger in this heavenly land. She enjoyed the sun but did not worship it. She loved her work and could never think of it as secondary to the hedonistic joys of Venice. Her body would never be a finely tuned instrument of muscle and dark brown skin, there was so much more to the world, so much to attend to.

Few of the beach people even noticed the slight, well-proportioned figure that walked quietly along the shore at sunset each night. She was aloof, a foreigner who sought the water's edge for comfort under a glowing moon instead of a searing sun. Faith was the audience of one who took delight in the performance of others but would never consider taking center stage. She had run to the upside-down beach world to lose herself, and she had succeeded.

Faith Karell, one of the privileged, an American princess, imbued with all the luxury that private enterprise could offer, had simply retreated to live in a world dedicated to battling criminals and crimes. She was unable to function in a frivolous and materialistic world anymore, unable to shut her eyes the way most people did.

The insistent, disgustingly cheery bell of her alarm suddenly broke her reverie. With a groan Faith turned toward the nightstand, attempting to disentangle herself from the multitude of covers that warmed her against the early-morning sea breeze.

"Damn." She cursed the sheets and the clock,

whose innocent large face stared at her, questioning her anger.

Finally freeing her arms, she reached for the alarm, missed it and sent a heavy volume of the *Federal Reporter* crashing to the polished wooden floor. Swinging her legs over the side of her tall brass bed, Faith sat for a moment, listening to the alarm, staring at the book.

Her cat poked its white head out from under the bed. "Don't worry, Bailiff," she sighed. "It's not a yelling day yet." The cat, cautious as usual, retreated back under the bed.

Faith picked up the book, turned off the alarm and switched on the stereo. The vibrant energy of Vivaldi filled the small house, mixing elegantly with the sounds from the beach. Faith hopped onto the floor, adjusting the old football jersey she wore for sleeping as she headed for the Spanish-tiled bathroom connected to her bedroom.

Though she would deny it, Faith looked better in the morning than most women after they were dressed. The jersey almost always caught in her skimpy silk panties in one corner or another. The large shirt accentuated her petite body and small, well-formed breasts, strong and perfectly proportioned legs, her tight derriere.

Long black curls fell in a tumble down her back, framing her face so she resembled a sleepy fairy princess. The face that looked into the mirror, glistening after its cold early-morning splash, appeared nondescript but for the large, luminous dark eyes. Naked in the first rays of daylight, her skin was soft and tawny,

needing only a bit of help from cosmetics to even out
the tone. As a young girl, Faith had not enjoyed the
rosy bloom that so many American girls came by naturally. Instead she had possessed that delicate creami-
ness of the long-ago beauty of magnolias. Only her
small thin lips interfered with the symmetry of her
face. Few even noticed this shortcoming when, with
skillful, unconscious application of her makeup, she
added the emphasis to her features that caused her
eyes to command attention and gave her skin a deep
and luminous glow.

Quickly discarding her jersey, she stepped into the
cavernous shower. The steaming water encased her,
woke her, drove the last vestige of sleep from her
mind and body. Finally accepting the start of the day,
Faith began to piece together the thoughts that had
drifted through her mind the night before, disturbing
her sleep.

The months of planning, investigating and waiting
would be culminated in less than two hours. Today
she would finally face her greatest challenge—the case
against Robert "Robo" Bennett would begin or end
with this suppression-of-evidence hearing.

Bennett headed the largest pornography ring in the
United States. He had made millions exploiting children of both sexes and exporting the films to lucrative
overseas markets. She and Mark MacMillan, the FBI
agent in charge of the case, had gathered enough evidence against Bennett to present a solid case and earn
a long-sought-after victory. The only thing that stood
in her way was Jim Stanten.

Stanten, the young, clever defense attorney, had

gained a reputation of his own. "Unbeatable," "The Devil's Darling." Newspapers across the country had heralded his performance as he traveled through the state defending shadowy figures and big white-collar criminals. Faith had followed his career closely. He was thirty-four, four years older than she. From the first, Faith had known that all her training was leading up to a confrontation with this man. Their backgrounds were so similar, yet he had chosen the road to money rather than the fight for justice. He had defended arsonists, fraud perpetrators—that was bad enough. But now, a pornographer! She thought it a terrible waste for someone so young and talented.

Sweeping her curls into a forties roll at the nape of her neck, she considered the man. His picture showed a serious person, never smiling for the camera, yet the expression was not surly. His brown wavy hair was carefully cut to frame his square face, giving the impression of a well-behaved little boy, trustworthy and kind—a plus with any jury. Dark brown eyes shone, alert, behind black wire-frame glasses that sat atop a short, slightly upturned nose. A full, tame mustache covered his upper lip. His lower lip was soft and full but hardly feminine. The whole effect, she thought, was carefully engineered to give the impression of honesty—a very important factor, considering his clients and a jury.

"This is one he's not going to get away with," Faith muttered, making her way to the large closet in the sunny bedroom, as she mulled over his credentials. Stanford Law School, clerk for a Supreme Court justice—impressive...disappointing. How could he defend people like Robert Bennett? Faith pulled a steel-gray silk suit and shell-pink blouse from their hangers.

"I might as well be his downfall." She sighed, feeling reluctant to fight this man for reasons she could not readily identify.

There in the privacy of her home, Faith was nervous. She had little use for her colleagues who chased the big dollars with no regard for the spirit of the law, much less the letter of it. Faith knew she would have to get a handle on Stanten quickly today, get a feel for his style, and figure out where her weak point was in his mind even before he identified it.

"Oh, Bailiff, this is what I've been waiting for," she said to the cat as she tied the soft bow of her blouse. "Wish me luck." The cat tipped its head, silently watching her pull on her slim gray pumps. Briefcase and car keys waited at the door. Gathering the tools of her trade, Faith headed toward the garage and gracefully swung her legs into the old VW. The car started smoothly and she backed out into the busy street, turned and headed toward the old stone courthouse eleven miles away, nestled in the heart of downtown Los Angeles.

A wisp of hair had escaped her ivory combs; her stocking showed the beginning of a run at her heel, yet unaware of these slight imperfections, intent on the problems at hand, she drove on, down the streets that would soon be melting under the L.A. sun. Jim Stanten was the only problem she thought about, and he would be with her in a cool, dark courtroom in just forty-five minutes.

The car seemed to fly over the streets and freeway as though it were somehow anxious to deposit its nervous driver at the appointed stop. Faith had been ten minutes early, time enough for a leisurely walk to the courthouse, but she could not seem to control her feet. Quickly she had moved with the hordes of government workers who made their way to the various buildings surrounding the civic center mall. Moments after leaving her car, Faith Karell walked quietly into the courtroom.

The silent, dark room was so familiar that Faith seldom took the time to admire it anymore. Now she sat conferring with Mark MacMillan at the prosecutor's table. There would be no spectators today quietly moving in a helter-skelter manner into the oak pews behind her. Twelve good men and true would not fill the raised jury box. There would be no young, inexperienced defense attorney who would stand, intimidated, beneath the great seal that hung like a dull, golden sun over the judge's bench. Today her mind was on the one man who would soon seat himself at the table for the defense.

"He'll be here any minute." Mark turned his wrist, nervously winding his watch, as he spoke. "If you don't counter this motion, we'll lose the best piece of evidence we've got."

"I know that. You know as well as I do this suppression motion is just a formality at most." Faith sounded convincing, but she was unsettled. The raid conducted by Mark's team of agents had been based on rather questionable information provided by one of Bennett's own men. Where the law was concerned, this might be a gray area, and she knew that Stanten had based his motion primarily on this point.

"I know Judge Hardison," she continued softly, almost reverently. "He's as anxious as we are to get Bennett. He'll be fair, but he'll help us all he can."

"I hope you're right, babe." His answer was offhand, but Faith couldn't help the involuntary stiffening of her body.

"Cut it out, Mark!" She hated his use of endearments, feeling it somehow compromised their professional relationship. And the few dinner dates they had had together did not constitute a personal relationship, at least not in her mind.

An almost imperceptible scraping of wood against marble cut short the lecture she was about to give him. Turning, she saw Jim Stanten enter the courtroom. He hesitated, briefcase in hand, standing like a statue in the gloom of the half-lit room, his right arm behind his back, the heavy wooden door slowly coming to rest on the hidden hand. He did not seem to move a muscle as the door closed on him. For a moment, only a moment, he stood framed by the polished wood, tall and unmoving.

"Hello." The greeting was more like a cheery announcement of his arrival. Faith winced. She had always thought it was an unspoken rule of the profession never to speak above a whisper in an empty courtroom, especially when addressing someone sitting at the counsel tables.

Mechanically she rose, pushing the short, swinging door that divided the spectator arena from the well and went to meet him. She hoped, somehow, by this action to calm him, quiet him, as he moved toward her. In an instant he was in front of her. As if drawn unwillingly to him, she took his hand. Hers trembled. Unnerved by the contact, she introduced herself.

"Mr. Stanten? Faith Karell." Her voice was hushed, professional; perhaps his would follow suit.

"Faith." He had not taken the hint. Worse yet, he addressed her by her first name. "I've heard a lot about you. Looks as if I'm in for quite a fight!"

He smiled, a glorious smile, and Faith flushed. A newspaper photo could never do him justice. He was not as tall as he first appeared—just under six feet, she guessed. His clothes were elegant but understated; they would never offend a jury by a show of wealth. His voice was open and bright, well-modulated and warm. Realizing her hand was still in his, she withdrew it, preceding him into the well.

"Jim Stanten, Mark MacMillan," Faith whispered as Mark rose to greet them.

"We've met in a way, Mr. Stanten," Mark said.

"Yes, I remember." The smile had faded slightly and Faith wondered at the change in attitude. She noticed the gleam of his starched white cuff as he offered his hand to Mark. That hand was strong, with flat pink nails; a fine blanket of light brown hair peeked from under the cuff. She shook her head, cleared her mind, cursing herself for the flush that was coming over her. Stanten turned suddenly, took a few steps and settled himself at the defense table. Faith slid into her chair, catching her stocking on the table leg.

"You all right?" Mark touched her arm lightly, confused by her demeanor.

"Sure. Of course," Faith answered vaguely, still contemplating her first meeting with Jim Stanten. He certainly had something, something Faith hadn't counted on. Charisma. Never before had she faced a defense attorney like him. He exuded confidence but was not overbearing. He was obviously intelligent and well-bred but didn't flaunt the fact. She couldn't resist glancing in his direction. He sat impassively reading the top page of a large sheaf of papers, his concentration total. Faith's jaw tightened. Charm is not going to win this time, she promised herself.

A panel suddenly opened in the wooden wall behind the bench. A tall black woman, delicate and creamy, entered the room and settled herself below the bench. In one graceful movement she placed her long fingers on a small machine ready to record the proceedings. The bailiff, an old man in a suit that appeared too large for him, followed her. Then Judge Hardison puffed along after his two assistants, his long, black robe giving him the appearance of a large, round piece of chocolate. His florid face and bald head were the cherry on top. Hardison was a happy man, giving the impression of someone easily swayed by a quick turn of a phrase, but Faith knew better. He was a fair judge but hard and unrelenting when an attorney failed to do his or her homework, failed to take the law seriously. Faith sat up straight.

*This is where he'll screw up,* she thought, a wry smile playing on her lips. *That carefree attitude won't cut the mustard with Hardison.*

"Good morning, counsels." There was a shifting of bodies as the judge addressed them. The court reporter quietly applied herself to her unusual typewriter, the long, thin tape beginning to edge out of the top of the machine as the judge spoke.

"Miss Karell, are you ready on behalf of the United States?" The judge peered over his bifocals and smiled at her.

"Yes, Your Honor." Faith rose for an instant, then settled back, upright in her chair.

"Mr. Stanten? This is the first time you've appeared before me." It was a statement, not a question.

"Yes, Your Honor." Jim Stanten was on his feet, his tone respectful—not intimidating, as Faith had hoped it would be. A pencil was suspended casually between the palms of his hands.

"I'm looking forward to witnessing your performance. Your record is surprisingly good, although I can't commend you on the choice of clients." The judge smiled. Faith was dismayed; he did not reveal any innate prejudice against Jim Stanten but, she realized, she would have expected nothing less.

"Every man is innocent until proven otherwise, Your Honor."

"Quite so, Mr. Stanten. Your client will not be joining us, I gather?"

"No, Your Honor, I have a waiver of my client's presence." Jim Stanten handed a piece of paper to the bailiff and then resumed his seat confidently.

Faith sat back more comfortably in the wooden chair. After that exchange she felt sure that Stanten would use the wrong approach somewhere along the way, alienating the judge for the duration of the long trial.

"Well, let's proceed." Hardison adjusted his glasses

on the tip of his nose and looked at the defense attorney. "Counsel," he continued, "I have read your papers in which the defense seeks to suppress from evidence the allegedly pornographic materials seized by the FBI in their search on the evening of July 27."

Stanten rose and strode to the podium. Placing his strong hands on either side of the polished mahogany stand, he leaned slightly forward and began to speak.

"As Your Honor knows, the agents obtained from Ms. Karell a search warrant for my client's premises on Moldonow Street based on hearsay from a rather unreputable source."

"Your Honor." Faith was on her feet, her voice betraying her impatience. "The raid in question was carried out on the stated evening, and thirteen crates of film and other matter depicting sexual activity between adults and children of all ages were found and confiscated on the basis of solid information," she continued, consciously controlling the strain in her voice. "These films were seized pursuant to probable cause by the magistrate of this court. And, as I'm sure Mr. Stanten is aware, the magistrate issues such warrants. I, as yet, have not been appointed to that position." She sat down, a small smile playing on her lips.

"This counsel," Stanten countered, "is well aware of the paperwork involved in the justice system, although I have heard rumors that the U.S. Attorney's office tends to view the magistrate as its personal rubber stamp." He grinned at her, unruffled.

"Now, now, Mr. Stanten." The judge chuckled. "You give far too much credit to the office of the U.S. Attorney."

Faith felt the color rise to her face. How could he? How could Hardison be taken in by this man?

"Continue, Mr. Stanten." The older man waved the younger on. Faith felt the reassuring pressure of Mark's arm on hers, and she was grateful for his presence.

Stanten cleared his throat. "Your Honor, as stated in my motion to suppress this evidence, you will note the informant is a convicted child molester of the most unreliable reputation. I suggest his reliability is, therefore, compromised and unusable. When requesting a warrant to search a respectable place of business should the magistrate consider such testimony?" He looked so sincere as he asked the question that even Faith was taken in, but only for a microsecond, then she reacted.

"Your Honor." Again she rose to her feet, fingers spread on the gleaming table. "As much as the government dislikes the use of such informants, it must be pointed out that Mr. Quarles, the gentleman in question, is in the employ of Mr. Stanten's client and that Mr. Stanten himself used Mr. Quarles as an expert witness in some of his more colorful trials. In short, the counsel's reliance on Mr. Quarles has been in evidence long before that of the government."

"That is true, Miss Karell," Stanten shot back, "but, Your Honor, what is really at question here is my client's rights under the Fourth Amendment of the Constitution. I firmly believe that the information supplied by Mr. Quarles is not sufficient grounds to violate Mr. Bennett's rights of search and seizure. I respectfully request suppression of the evidence in question." His response was as quick and professional as any Faith had ever heard.

Faith drew in her breath sharply, ready to counter his argument, but was cut short by the judge.

"Counsels, I have thoroughly familiarized myself with the motion in my possession. I have enjoyed, however, familiarizing myself with you two before the jury selection and trial. This should prove to be a most exciting experience." He cleared his throat and removed his glasses.

"Unfortunately, Mr. Stanten, I believe you have trifled a bit with the court's time. There are no grounds for suppression of the evidence in question. Ms. Karell, you may proceed with the preparation of your case. Motion denied." The gavel struck sharply. Judge Hardison rose. It was over.

Her briefcase was packed, and Faith turned on her heel, rushing through the door before the judge had disappeared through the hidden panel to his chambers. She had won, yet she was furious with herself, the judge, with Stanten for being so cool. Faith had been so sure he would fall on his face.

Mark followed her but not quickly enough. The elevator closed before he could reach her, leaving him looking at the scarred panels of the ancient door.

"Women!" he muttered to himself as he watched the numbers change above the elevator. Turning toward the main entrance of the courthouse, he made his way to the coffee shop on Main Street where he was sure to find the company of other agents.

The elevator rose to the tenth floor. The office was a madhouse—phones ringing, secretaries hurrying here and there—as Faith made her way, as unobtrusively as possible, toward her office.

"How'd it go?" Darcy, her secretary, had spotted her.

"We won," Faith called flatly over her shoulder, never breaking her stride, and hurried on to the refuge of her large but shabby office. Here she breathed a little easier. The diplomas and prints added a personal touch to the dilapidated office; a large fern provided a bit of brightness. Shutting the door securely, Faith made her way to the large orange Naugahyde chair behind the desk. Her small frame seemed to shrink away as she settled herself into the well-worn seat.

Faith sat, her mind wandering, her anger abating as the minutes ticked by. She knew her reactions had been childish. Somewhere in the back of her mind was a thought that she couldn't—wouldn't—allow to surface.

Finally it was there—clear, bothersome, totally irritating. Jim Stanten was an attractive man. Her hand could still feel the warmth of his when they shook hands. Her mind's eye could still see the lovely white teeth—a slight overbite making his smile seem boyish and disarming.

So many years, and now, when it was so important not to remember, this man walks into the courtroom and reminds her she's a woman. A man like that! A high-priced ambulance chaser. A man who sells his skill, albeit brilliant, to the highest bidder, no matter what his crime. Ever since he had won his first case, defending the head of a local drug ring, he had been on the front pages. Jim Stanten could somehow swing even an open-and-shut case his client's way. Faith could not deny it was due to his constant digging for facts. But once those facts were unearthed, Stanten could twist them until any witness wouldn't know what he had seen or heard.

*I'm going to take him down a peg,* she thought, *along with Bennett.* Smiling, she leaned over her desk, picking up the first file she found. Faith felt better. She would work until she was ready for the battle. She would be so well prepared there would be no way in hell he could beat her. Consciously, Faith shoved the disconcerting image of his handsome face to the far reaches of her mind as she began her afternoon of work.

Five hours later the sun still hung lazily in the late afternoon sky. Its angle was perfectly set to blaze into her eyes as Faith worked, so she adjusted the old venetian blinds to darken the room and turned on the unflattering fluorescent light instead. The last few hours had been like a shot in the arm because she had been able to work uninterrupted. Just as she was contemplating an early escape and quiet dinner, Faith heard the phone ring, muffled by the books and papers that covered it. Sifting through the rubble, Faith found the ugly black telephone that angrily called attention to itself and pressed her private extension.

"Hello, mom." She had never given the number out to anyone else, and the assistants were well protected in matters of private phone numbers, so she knew it had to be her mother on the other end of the line.

"Faith? How about a truce? Dinner tonight?" The voice that greeted her was soft and very masculine.

"How did you get this number?" she demanded as shock took over; she recognized the voice.

Jim Stanten chuckled—a soft, low, delightful sound—at the other end of the line.

# *Chapter Two*

"You all right, honey?" Darcy waddled into the shabby office, her bright print dress swaying with each step as she headed for the chair opposite Faith's desk. "Hey, Faith, are you in there?" the woman continued, trying to gain her employer's attention.

"Yeah, sure, Darcy, I'm fine," Faith answered, her voice hollow and far away as the chair in which Darcy settled herself released a plaintive sigh through a rip in the seat cushion. Darcy's stubby fingers played with the stuffing protruding from the side of the chair as she looked into Faith's concerned face.

"Now, I know better than that. Why don't you tell me all about it and get it over with? It'll save us both a lot of time. Otherwise I'll have to keep asking until you finally say something. Come on, what's got your gut? Is it this case?" The younger woman's face relaxed into a smile as she looked at Darcy's sparkling black eyes. It never ceased to amaze her that Darcy's pixie face could be set on such a large body.

"Well, you might say it's the case. I just had a phone call from Jim Stanten—" Before she could finish, Faith was interrupted by the older woman, her hands flying to her perfectly coiffed Afro.

"Why, that idiot! Is he starting to bother you already? What kind of tricks is that shyster playing? From now on you let me answer all of your calls until this thing is over, do you hear?" Faith loved it when Darcy flew into one of her fits of fury, her small head bobbing up and down on her large body, her eyes bulging with anger.

"It's not that kind of problem," she answered laughingly, "at least I don't think it is. So far there hasn't been any harassment. He just asked me to dinner tonight." Why was she embarrassed, Faith wondered. She hadn't done anything to be ashamed of, but she flushed under Darcy's scrutiny.

Darcy's smile covered her girlish face, lighting up her features like a Christmas tree. "That's the kind of harassment I like to hear about! His picture in those files looks mighty inviting." Faith could hardly believe that only moments ago the woman before her had been ready to do battle with Jim Stanten. What a strange woman she was, able to turn her emotions off and on like that.

"Inviting or not," Faith retorted, "I just don't think it's all that ethical to be seeing him. After all, he's defending that creep Bennett. I know that we're only supposed to be adversaries in the courtroom, but from everything I've heard about him, he's a snake." A snake who made her feel like Eve in the Garden, she thought involuntarily.

She could still remember the impact he had had on her in the courtroom and, now, trying to sound righteous, she felt as though Darcy could read her every thought. Could the other woman guess what was really in the back of her mind? But Darcy hadn't even noticed Faith's reaction in her excitement; the blush had gone unnoticed.

"You mean you turned him down? You haven't been out in ages except for that MacMillan person. When are you going to get on the stick, ma'am? It's time you had yourself a little fling!" Darcy was always trying to play matchmaker, but this time she really didn't know what she was saying... or so Faith told herself.

"Darcy," she admonished her secretary, "he only asked me to dinner. That hardly constitutes a fling!" Looking askance at the woman, she tried her best to sound indignant and was only rewarded with a dazzling white smile. In a minute she, too, was giggling at the absurdity of the situation.

How many prosecutors did she know who fought like tigers against a defense attorney in the courtroom only to meet as friends over drinks an hour later? Perhaps she was beginning to take things too seriously.

"Well, actually, I accepted. I just don't know why," she admitted sheepishly, feeling like a rowdy child who had been caught drawing pictures on the wall, "but this is to be kept between you and me, do you understand?" The last thing Faith needed was for the entire office to be gossiping about a nonexistent affair. But, watching Darcy, she knew the plea had fallen on deaf ears.

"Okay, okay." Darcy raised her hand in mock fear at Faith's command. Faith was immediately sure that

it would be less than five minutes before every em-
ployee of the office from the lowliest secretary to the
U.S. Attorney himself was aware of the dinner date.

"Now, I mean it," she reiterated, trying to sound
strong and convincing. Darcy had been with her too
long to fall for the act and simply raised her great bulk
out of the small chair and headed slowly to the door,
muttering all the way.

"I'd say it's going to be some night. This office
hasn't had anything good to gossip about for ages.
But, if you say so...not a word to anybody, I swear."
Faith sat quietly until she could no longer hear the
hilarious soliloquy the woman carried on as she
headed down the hall.

Glancing at her watch, she noted the time and decided to call it a day. Jim was going to pick her up at
seven, and the traffic had been miserable all week.
She might as well head home a bit early and have a
little time to herself before she had to dress for the
evening. Ignoring the mess of papers and books on
her desk, she drew her lizard bag from the bottom
drawer of her desk, slowly pulled on her suit jacket
and left the office, not noticing the curious looks from
the secretarial pool.

Quickly she made her way through the heat-choked
hallway of the old building, tapped her foot while she
waited for the ancient elevator, and finally strode
through the front door of the Federal Hall of Justice.
Even though it was early, people were already jostling
each other on the street as they made their way to the
many parking lots surrounding the courthouse. With a
grateful sigh Faith finally made it to her little car, in-

serted the key into the ignition and pulled out onto
Sunset to make her way to the San Diego Freeway,
the biggest parking lot in the world.

"Damn." Faith ran her hands through the damp
wings of her rolled hair. "I've got to get a new car. Air
conditioning would definitely be a plus and make this
a whole lot easier."

Craning her head out the window, she noted the
never-ending line of cars in front of her; she was
greeted by the same scene when she looked behind.
There was probably an accident up ahead that had
brought the normally slow flow of Los Angeles traffic
to a screeching, annoying halt. She'd been on the
freeway for thirty minutes already. So much for time
to herself. The late afternoon sun cut through her
windshield just below her sun visor, and her eyes
burned with the fumes from the hundreds of exhaust
pipes and heavy blanket of ever-present smog that
hung over the city.

Los Angeles was a strange city. Its climate was
clement most of the year, but when visitors came in
September or October, they were often treated to the
surprise that the hottest part of the summer was actually the beginning of fall. Sometimes when the heat
was coupled with the strange and destructive Santa
Ana winds, the whole city resembled a little touch of
purgatory.

Laying her head back on the seat of her crotchety
Volkswagen, Faith continued to massage her temples
as she thought about the evening to come.

Subconsciously she knew she was rationalizing her
acceptance when she told herself that she would be

able to gain an insight into her legal adversary. After all, a leisurely dinner, drinks, a flamboyant man who was more than willing to discuss his cases if she could believe what she read in the papers . . . what better way to discover the chink in his armor?

Besides, she would get a free meal in the bargain. The thought of cooking on a steaming day never did appeal to her very much. And on the salary the government paid, she had to take advantage of every opportunity to dine out. It was a comforting thought that the evening might be considered a strategic session rather than a dinner date, though. Faith did not acknowledge the thrill that ran through her body each time she envisioned his face, his subtle body movements, his wonderful voice.

Inch by inch the car moved forward. The searing asphalt stretched almost endlessly before her, the honking cars seeming to divide and multiply before her eyes.

An hour later Faith breathed a sigh of relief as the little car pulled into the alley behind her house and settled in the ramshackle garage. Closing the heavy door, Faith shut out for one more day the grime and noise of downtown Los Angeles and headed through her small garden toward the house, reveling in the clean, fresh sea air that greeted her.

Bailiff acknowledged her casually, wrapping his tail about her leg as she entered. Then, gracefully moving toward the corner of the kitchen, he signaled his desire for dinner.

"All right," she snapped at the cat, her long drive having destroyed any semblance of a good mood, "no need to be so high and mighty."

She would have to calm down, forget the traffic and the office and concentrate on her frame of mind. Dinner tonight would be a working meeting, and Faith intended to gather enough information about Mr. Jim Stanten to blow him out of the legal water when they finally came to trial.

Automatically Faith reached for a can of cat food, yawned as she listened to the whirr of the electric can opener, spooned the food into the battered old dish and left the cat nibbling happily at his tasty treat.

It wasn't until she had poured herself a glass of wine, kicked off her shoes and fallen onto the bed that Faith began to wonder, not about her reasons for accepting the dinner invitation, but about Jim Stanten's motives for asking her.

She had never met the man until that morning and, from everything she had read or heard about him, there were a number of women in his life. So why her? Why tonight? After all, he had the resources of one of the biggest law firms in Los Angeles behind him. He would know everything about her before they went to trial, right down to the brand of panty hose she wore. What could he possibly hope to gain from their meeting that night?

The questions played over and over again in her mind. Her father had always told her to beware of men like Jim Stanten, they were poison in business. Smooth, debonair and too smart for their own good. Her father should know. He was one of them and could play the games better than anyone she knew.

He was the kind of man, though, who had played the games of international law for a reason. The Depression had taken its toll on his family, and after putting himself through law school, talking and working his way to the top of his profession, her father knew his wife and daughters had had the one thing he wanted most in the world—security. Even now, in his comfortable retirement, he was still called upon to negotiate deals between the powerful and wealthy of the world. Not just with people, but for entire countries.

Faith could understand that kind of drive. And while she admired her father's legal mind, she could not follow in his footsteps, which led to using the law for personal gain. Each of them respected what the other did, but neither could understand it. Neither could imagine using the law in any way but the one he or she had chosen. But Faith had learned her lessons well from her father, and she was determined not to forget them that night.

Draining her glass of the last crystalline drop of wine, she threw her feet over the side of the bed and hopped onto the floor, enjoying the feel of the smooth wood as she made her way into the bathroom. With the faucets turned on, the ancient bathtub filling, Faith knew she had about five minutes before she would have to stave off the overflow.

Like so many things in Faith's life now, there was a certain comfort in those small things that could be depended upon, such as warm, soothing water filling a tub in exactly five minutes. Just enough time to move to the sink and remove all traces of the mascara she wore. Just enough time to remove the confining pins that held her luxurious hair so severely at the nape of her neck. How reassuring to know that the small things in life went on, yet how predictable, how boring, all those small things seemed tonight.

Turning back to the tub, Faith quickly turned off the water and made her way into the bedroom. Bailiff padded about the room, his dinner finished, wrapping his long, graceful tail about the legs of her dressing table, then he crouched and sailed in one sweeping motion through the air to land with supreme confidence atop the satin comforter.

"There isn't any way I'm going to keep you off that bed, is there, Bailiff?" Faith asked absentmindedly of the cat who had curled into a luscious ball of white fur, as she stepped out of her hose and loosened the zipper of her skirt.

Long ago Faith had stopped worrying about her insistent habit of chatting with Bailiff as she moved about the house. Now discarding each tailored piece of clothing into a heap on the floor, she continued her one-sided conversation.

"I don't know, you dumb cat. Why do you think he did it? It could be that I am truly an irresistible creature, full of sex appeal and mystery." She smiled awkwardly, raising her arms and piling her hair atop her head as she surveyed her slim figure, turning back and forth in front of the standing mahogany mirror. Making a face at her reflection, she decided once and for all that could not possibly be the reason. Giving up her game, Faith stepped into her bath and luxuriated in its scented warmth. Again and again, thoughts of Jim Stanten's ulterior motives for the invitation came back to haunt her.

There was no denying the attraction Faith felt for

Jim Stanten. Not only was he a good-looking man, but there was a certain panache about the way he handled himself in the courtroom. He moved with a grace that Faith only could wish to possess. His voice was modulated, pleasant, almost endearing, and he would be dangerous in front of a jury because of these qualities. She couldn't help but admire that; she couldn't help but wish she exuded the same confidence.

But she didn't and she knew it. No matter what case she was working on, Faith's delivery betrayed the extreme sense of righteousness she felt. There was almost too much conviction in her voice. She could never sweet-talk a jury into the proper verdict, never ease them down the right path of thinking. She would give anything to melt into Jim Stanten and find out what it felt like to be so at ease with oneself in those rooms where judgment was passed on people's lives every day of the year. His confidence was exciting, no matter how she tried to deny it.

But Faith had to remember what he stood for. He was the lowliest of the low, Mr. Stanten was. His defense was not of the innocent or the underdog. He cared nothing for the rights of victims. Jim Stanten cared about money, publicity and power.

"Two can play at this game, Mr. Stanten, but only one can win, and I intend to be the one," she muttered to herself as she stepped out of the tub and toweled herself. With a shake of her head she walked, her step firm and deliberate, into the bedroom and began riffling through the contents of her closet.

Suit after suit passed through her fingers...gray, blue, brown...pinstripes, herringbones, solids. All sensible fabrics and cuts. Very businesslike but not very appropriate. What she needed was something alluring, something that would throw him off guard. She knew his type, and there was no harm in playing the opposition's game as long as one remembered one was playing.

Sticking her head back into the deep closet, Faith groped again. Finally, she found it, the black silk. It had been years since she had worn it. The last time was when her father was made chairman of the board of Lectricon. Silently she blessed him and his success as she slipped the plastic bag off the whisper-thin silk and laid it on the bed.

"Off you go, Bailiff," she said as she shooed the cat onto the floor. Cat hair would never do tonight; everything had to be perfect.

It was a game of wits, Faith kept telling herself as she applied her makeup until her face shone with a glow she had forgotten existed in her. The nagging deep in the recesses of her mind was pushed back until it hardly existed. But, exist it did. The thought deep inside her, the idea that she was anxious for Jim Stanten's attention and that she looked forward to their evening together, was still there. But with the last flick of mascara, the little annoying thought had all but been tucked away in a quiet little corner of her head.

She questioned whether to wear her hair up, but thought, no, Jim would be the type that would like it impractical. Winding her tresses about her curling iron, she added touches of fullness to her naturally wavy hair until it stood back from her face like a wild, untamed mane.

Ten minutes later she was ready. Her slight figure
was made svelte by the dolman sleeves of the dress as
they flowed into the slim, straight skirt. Opera-length
pearls added a touch of sophistication.

"Well, dear Bailiff"—she smiled into the mirror as
she spoke—"this is the best I can do; let's hope it's
good enough." Sighing, she turned out the bedroom
light and went to wait for Jim Stanten in the living
room.

For the tenth time Faith pulled the curtains back
from the picture window in her living room and
scanned the street outside. Nothing. Glancing at the
clock above the mantel, she noted the time: He was
already half an hour late, and her courage was waning.
She paced the floor, back and forth, switching the tape
in her stereo for the third time.

Was his timing intentional? Is that what he wanted
her to do? Wait and worry and wonder? If so, the ploy
was working. Then Faith jumped, startled by the
three-tiered chime of the doorbell. Taking a deep
breath, she smoothed her skirt and glanced into the
mirror one last time. Throwing back her shoulders,
she made her way to the door, hesitating for only a
second before she switched on the outside light and
opened the door.

"Hi." He had been looking at the street, hands in
his pockets, but now turned to face her as he heard
the door open.

Faith was stunned; she felt like a fool. Jim Stanten
was dressed in a pair of beautifully fitted jeans, un-
structured sport jacket and open-neck shirt. He
smelled as though he had just taken a refreshing walk

on the beach, his after-shave was so light and delicate as he walked past her into the living room.

"May I come in?" Faith was too embarrassed to move for a moment. She hadn't even thought to ask where they were going for dinner; she had simply assumed that someone like him would want to really show off. Recovering from her shock, she knew she had to play out the scene she was dressed for. Faith was going to be the epitome of grace and charm and sophistication if it killed her. There was time enough for the becoming blush that was rising to her cheeks, and she fought back the color.

"Of course you may," she said, attempting to sound cool and unruffled as he turned to look at her.

"You look lovely. I'm afraid I'm a bit underdressed. I hope you'll forgive me." The sincerity in his voice seemed genuine and only served to confuse Faith even more. She hadn't expected the gentlemanly gesture.

"Thank you, but I'm afraid I should have realized that my outfit would be a little dressy. Sometimes I tend to forget how casual Los Angeles is." Faith smiled deprecatingly, more to herself than to him. She really was a throwback. All those years of traveling with her father, living in Paris and Rome when he was on extended cases, had taught her the European way of living. Women dressed for dinner occasions. Faith still had a wardrobe of hats and gloves from those days, which she never used but held on to anyway. As though he were reading her mind, he commented.

"That's right. You have lived all over the world. I

guess L.A. seems like small time to you." Did she read a bit of sarcasm in his tone? Or was she simply hoping it was there? Faith was ashamed of herself; it was so unlike her to search for a confrontation.

"You seem to know a lot about me...." She challenged him to tip his hand, admit that his little researchers at MacManus, Price and Weeks had done their jobs properly, informing him of all her likes and dislikes. Oh, if only she could have the same resources at her disposal, she wouldn't be going through this charade...or would she? To her dismay he reacted coolly, never missing a beat in the conversation, politely ignoring her comment.

"Shall we go?" His hand was placed lightly on her arm, his closeness disconcerting.

"Certainly. Just let me get my purse." With that Faith hurried into the bedroom, conscious of him appraising every inch of her back as she left. Her eyes flew about the room before she spied the black silk bag she had left on the bed. For a minute she clutched it to her, breathing deeply as she did so, collecting her thoughts.

It had been a long time since she had experienced the warm swelling deep in the pit of her stomach. Faith was amazed at herself. Five minutes with this man and she was reduced to confusion beyond compare. She would have to be very careful as the evening progressed.

"Here we go, Bailiff; wish me luck," she whispered to the cat and went to meet Jim Stanten.

Faith's disappointment was evident when Jim expertly maneuvered the black Porsche into the last parking space in front of the small restaurant. They had driven past the elegant eating places of Beverly Hills and onto Santa Monica Boulevard. On and on they went, while Jim chattered away about sports, cars and law school and Faith responded with a nod here and a casual response there. She had been too curious to see where they would end up spending the evening to pay much attention to the conversation. Now she knew.

While Jim got out of the sleek car and came around the back to open the door for Faith, she surveyed the situation. They were in the no-man's-land of Santa Monica Boulevard—the outskirts of Los Angeles proper. The neighborhood was run-down and ominous, deserted except for a trio of teenagers standing on the street corner listening to a boom box, which Faith assumed was stolen, and a young woman, more than likely a prostitute, dressed in satin shorts and black boots worn badly at the heel.

Directly in front of her was an anonymous-looking doorway, above which a lighted Pepsi-Cola sign hung. It was the only light visible on the street. All the other storefronts were black and locked with sliding barred gates against the unfortunate inhabitants of the neighborhood. Above the door someone had painted the words Studio Grill in bright cherry red. From the looks of the sign, the artist's hand had either been untrained or unsteady from drink at the time the job was completed.

Faith felt a rush of warm air as the car door was opened. The air-conditioning had been so pleasant that she had forgotten the misery of the September heat.

"Here we are." She looked up at Jim's smiling face. He was so polite, so normal, that Faith found herself wishing he was anyone but her legal adversary.

"Where are we?" she demanded, her earlier resolve to appear unruffled, no matter what, melting under the force of her rising anger at his obvious poor taste in bringing her to a place like this. Refusing the hand he offered, she swung her shapely legs out and over the low, deep leather seat and onto the cracked sidewalk.

"Is this one of your client's little hangouts?" Her sarcastic, accusatory tone did not escape him, and his face clouded, but he ignored her comment. Faith smiled, feeling a little better for reminding him of his position.

"No, I promise there are no miserable criminals lying in wait inside the door. No harm will come to you tonight," he said, his cheerfulness returning instantly, it seemed. Taking her arm and pushing open the small, weather-ravaged door, he guided her into the establishment and added cockily, "Unless you want some harm to come to you."

Faith shot him an imperious glance, ignoring the obvious innuendo of his remark, but the look soon melted into a charming smile as she surveyed the room about her. It was fabulous. No, more than fabulous.

Quiet conversation floated about the room couched on a cloud of harp music. Couples sat at small tables scattered about, each covered with a pink tablecloth the color of a perfect opal. A single rose adorned each table, and antique salt and pepper salvers glistened by

the crystal vases. The walls were covered in a beautiful damask tinged with tones of pink, rose and hunter
green. Even the people dining and talking casually in
the lovely little restaurant were beautiful, not the kind
one saw walking the streets of Beverly Hills or roller
skating by the beach. These people were somehow
different; they were only interested in their dining
partners, not anyone who opened the door. Los Angeles was funny that way. Even when out with someone, you always felt as though your escort wasn't
paying attention to you—but to everyone around you,
and never the one person he should be interested in.

She was hardly conscious of Jim's hand around her
shoulder until he spoke quietly into her ear, brushing
her dark tresses with his lips. "Still disappointed?" he
asked, teasing her.

"I . . ." What could she say? Had she been so trans-
parent? Or so rude as to let her disappointment show?

"Of course not. This is absolutely lovely. I do
apologize sincerely." Her voice was quiet and contrite.

"That's all right," he answered as Faith turned her
luminous eyes upon him. He hesitated for an instant,
then continued, "Faith, do you think we could start
over again? I've had the feeling for the last half hour
that you really don't want to be here with me. I'd like
to think I'm wrong."

Faith studied his face in the half light of the track
bulbs and flickering candles. *He is handsome,* she
thought. His skin was beautiful, clear and young,
though she knew he was older than she. Why not forget what she was for an evening? Tonight she would

be a woman, not the lawyer who was to destroy this man in court if she could.

"Yes," she replied hesitantly, "you are wrong." She was almost ashamed of the throaty tone of her voice. It was so unlike her. Did she sound too willing, too eager to prove that she was more than a government lawyer?

The pressure of his hand on her arm burned through the thin, slippery silk of her dress. Faith was mesmerized by the merry eyes that looked into hers, sparkling without his glasses to hide their depth. She was hardly breathing, trying to control the shiver that was running up her spine. He seemed like any other man on a first date. Couldn't he feel it? Did he not feel the spirit-stirring pain of attraction when he touched her, too?

Her preoccupation with the man standing so close to her was interrupted by the mute maître d' who simply bowed and led them to a table deep in the heart of the long room. There, surrounded by palms and prints, Faith settled back to watch the man named Jim Stanten.

"Thank you." He raised his eyes to the white-clad waiter who quietly placed a snifter of brandy in front of each of them.

"Now, you were saying?" His sable eyes had once again turned back to her and, once again, as he had unconsciously done throughout the evening, he appraised her with obvious enjoyment.

"It wasn't anything too terribly important, just expounding on the horrible waste of funds when we are forced to try and retry cases because of some technicality." She threw her hands up in a graceful gesture as though brushing away a silken strand of hair freed by a spring breeze.

Faith felt wonderful, relaxed. She found it hard to believe that she was enjoying herself as much as she was. There had been nothing earthshaking about Jim Stanten—at least not from a professional standpoint. She had found nothing that could help her once they faced each other in the courtroom. He had been courteous, charming and witty all evening. Dinner had been exquisite: heart of palm salad, squab with raspberries and the lightest cheesecake Faith had ever tasted. Through the aperitifs and the wine they had traded law school stories, his attentiveness lulling Faith into friendship. Sitting, as they did, across from each other, she felt safe. There had been no attempt to hold her hand, no more innuendo, no condescending conversation about women and law. In short it had been a most delightful evening, the best she had spent in over a year. Ah, but her guard was down. She had forgotten the man sitting across from her was to be her adversary. Now, over brandy, the restaurant almost devoid of other people, they had begun to venture into dangerous conversation, laced with questions that hit at the heart of Faith's life, the core of her existence. But she could not see the warning signs or, if she did, she ignored them.

"But," he answered, "not all retrials are based on technicalities. Some are absolutely mandatory in order to see justice done." He was leaning closer to her now, and, once again, she was conscious of the aftershave he wore.

"Justice!" Faith scoffed, good-naturedly still. "I wouldn't think that you would be terribly interested in that, considering your client list and your firm. Why, they're known for defending anyone with enough money."

She was unaware of the almost imperceptible change in him. Had she been in total control of her senses, she would have noted the fine shading of his eyes, the calm set of his mouth.

"I'm very interested in justice...to an extent. I refuse to let it govern my life when there is nothing I can do about it, but I do hate to see a gross miscarriage." Then, as quickly as he had leaned into her, he was gone, surveying her with interest as he settled back in the velvet chair.

A warning bell sounded in Faith's mind. No longer were they simply a man and woman having a late supper together. Things had changed, and she felt as though she had been blind-sided by a well-placed rap on the jaw. Every nerve was alive, standing at attention, waiting for the next blow, ready to thrust or parry as the need arose.

"But how often does that happen?" Faith queried carefully, wondering where the conversation was leading. "Certainly when it does, there are avenues available to rectify it."

"Possibly." He seemed preoccupied now but not with her. "For instance, what would you think of an agent who perjured himself? Wouldn't you call a conviction on that note a gross miscarriage of justice?"

"Certainly I would! I imagine that a case like that would be pursued until the guilty party was made to answer for it." Her blind faith in the system was so evident that Jim Stanten could not resist following up on the lead.

"What if the perjury managed to put away one of the most hated criminals known to the Justice Department?" he went on, his voice taking on that deceiving gentleness one experiences just before the final explosion of a tactful cross examination.

"Well, then, it still would not be justified. If the case couldn't stand on its own merits, then it shouldn't have come to trial in the first place." Her anger was rising; he was trying to bait her.

"You know MacMillan? I think he's on this case for you right now." She nodded her head in reply to his question, her lips parted to answer, but he went on, never missing a beat.

"Perhaps you heard of the case I handled about a year ago, Grogerzio? Well, your friend MacMillan perjured himself. What do you say about that?" A half smile played on his lips as he tapped his chin with one perfectly manicured finger.

Faith's eyes blazed and her breath came in short bursts. How dare he accuse Mark of anything so low? Who did he think he was? She rose quickly from the table, her napkin fluttering to her feet unnoticed.

"How dare you... you high-priced flunky! How dare you make that kind of accusation! If you spent half as much time with the agents as you do maintaining your playboy image, you would know that that is absolutely absurd!" The air about them fairly crackled, ignited by her anger.

Mark MacMillan was one of the best agents around.

He was cautious, never overstepping his bounds, never giving a judge any reason to throw the case out of court because of sloppy work, and now this idiot had the audacity to cite Mark for a crime she could not even comprehend. Like a lioness she rose to defend her partner.

Jim had also risen to face her and now put a hand out toward her as though he would try to restrain her physically.

"Don't touch me," she hissed at him through clenched teeth. Her righteous anger would have been evident to anyone around her, yet subconsciously Faith was afraid she might falter in her momentum if he were to make contact with her. She had not forgotten the thrill his touch seemed to bring to her, how every pore of her skin seemed to open and drink in the warmth of his hands. She didn't want to be reminded of the sweetness she had found in him during the last hours as she continued her tirade.

"When you work the way we do...understaffed, underpaid, through long hours of investigation, then you tell me about MacMillan and perjury. Until you start practicing real law instead of offering your services to the highest bidder, don't you tell me what you think you know. Until then, the only time I want to see you is in court. Good night, Mr. Stanten!"

She pushed past him, hitting her thigh on the sharp edge of the table. Aware that his eyes followed her as she stormed out of the restaurant, Faith refused to give in to the pain that was coursing through her leg. Had she turned back, she would have seen Jim

Stanten casually settle the check before slowly turning toward the door to follow her.

Instead, Faith pushed the small door open with a resounding thud as it hit the wall of the building outside. The blast of oppressive hot air that hit her as she stepped into the silent street only fueled her anger as she felt the instantaneous perspiration begin to bead on her body, sinking into the delicate fabric of her dress. She flung her head left and right, searching the silent street.

*Damn,* she thought, involuntarily stamping her foot and sending a shooting pain through her leg. *If only this was New York, I could be in a cab and on my way.* But there were no cabs, no buses, and in this part of town, it was dangerous to be caught on the streets late at night, especially dressed as she was. Tears of frustration began welling in her eyes. She was tired and lonely, disappointed and hurt by the man inside. All was silent; then she heard him behind her.

"You can't get home without me, you know." Faith whirled about, her hair flying over her face. Jim Stanten stood lounging against the doorwell of the grill, smiling at her as though nothing had happened.

"You're good, aren't you; you're really good!" Faith heard her voice rising to a scream as the shrill tones echoed through the empty streets.

"I've been told so," he answered, smiling rakishly at her as he moved closer.

"You are disgusting! You almost had me fooled. I applaud you, Mr. Stanten; your acting is beyond reproach. I can see why you win so many cases." He stood before her; closer and closer he leaned toward her as though, at any moment, he might kiss her. "I won't fall for it, buddy. I know your kind. And don't think your little play on words got by me. You're not dealing with some bubble-headed blonde from Beverly Hills, you know. I don't think it's funny and I don't like the way you do business." Her voice was frantic, and she took a deep breath, readying herself again, but he stopped her before she could control her emotions.

"That still doesn't change the fact that you're stuck here, does it?" His calm attitude only increased her anger, driving her crazy, and she wished she could wipe that insipid smile from his face.

"Now, do you want to get into the car or shall I leave you right here?" Faith stood her ground, her feet planted firmly on the decrepit sidewalk, panting for breath, trying to decide what to do.

"All right." His hand reached out and took her gently but firmly by the arm, spinning her around to face the car. "I'll help you make the decision."

With that, he pushed her across the short walk to the car and opened the door in one swift movement. Before Faith knew what had happened, she was settled into the tufted leather seat, the door closed firmly behind her. Crossing her arms she sat back fuming and turned her head to look out the window as Jim started the ominous-looking car with a roar and sped off toward the beach and Faith's home.

"You can't stop talking to me forever," he said as he downshifted into second, making the turn gracefully onto Pacific Coast Highway. "Why don't we make up and be friends?'' As he shifted once again into third, his hand brushed lightly against her thigh, sending a shiver through her body.

Faith moved in the seat, hugging her arms closer to her chest, praying that she would see the little pink house any moment now. She couldn't stand it anymore; she had to get out of the car—he was too close. Now she knew what a dangerous man he really was; he was too good, too smooth, and she would have to be wary of him once they started the trial. Tonight she would have to be wary of his physical presence. It seemed that even the slightest contact with him made her forget everything—her anger, her concern over his accusations, everything. And the danger of the realization made her shiver.

''I don't want to be friends. I just want to get home,'' she answered sullenly.

''Well, one more turn and you're there.'' With that the little car spun around a corner and he pulled to a screeching halt in front of her bungalow. Faith clumsily searched for the handle on the door.

''Where in the hell is the latch? These are such stupid cars!'' Her hand ran over the smooth, leather-covered door. *Just like him,* she thought, *all that money and he wasted it on a stupid foreign car.* Her frustration was growing as she sat in the dark confines of the Porsche.

''Here,'' he said simply as he reached across her and flipped the hidden handle, opening the door. His hand, free now, rested on her seat, and his face was precariously close to hers, his body forming a warm, living prison about her.

"Faith, I am sorry I upset you so much." Jim's voice was low and soft, his eyes as they looked into hers were sincere. "But I didn't lie. I know what I know."

For an instant she was silent, fighting back the feeling that was beginning to rise in her as he seemed to inch ever closer, trying to remember the indignation she should be feeling over his accusation.

"Can you prove it?" she demanded, losing the conviction in her voice as she attempted to return his unwavering gaze.

"Not yet." He shook his head slightly, then smiled. "But that doesn't mean it isn't true. You're acting like judge and jury, condemning me before you've even thought about it or checked my story out."

"Let me out of here,' she asked quietly, afraid to carry the conversation any further, afraid that he might convince her it was true. "Now, please," she begged.

"Do you despise me so much that you won't even give me a fair hearing? I thought you had a more finely tuned sense of justice than that," he commented, not moving.

"Look, I know what you are. Hell, half the attorneys in Los Angeles are out for a buck, but that doesn't give you the right to question the way real law works. Now, if your little fling for tonight is over, I want to get out of this car. It was really stupid of us to get together in the first place so will you please let me out!" She hit the last words hard, her voice cold.

Faith heard the deep sigh of the leather as he moved in his seat, and she breathed a sound of relief.

There was going to be no more argument. This was the end of the evening and the end of anything that might have been. But tinged with the gratefulness that he was going to be a gentleman and let her out of the car was a disturbing tremor of sadness that ran through her heart and mind. He had made her feel so like a desirable woman until that vicious accusation.... Why did it have to be like this? Why did men always have to ruin everything?

Her relief was cut short before she could think another thought, before she could take another breath. He had moved his strong hand from the seat and captured her face, pulling it close to him, covering her lips with his as he leaned over the console.

Taken by surprise, Faith acted automatically, melting into him, forgetting her anger, denying their differences, enjoying the soft bristles of his mustache as they sensually tickled her upper lip. There, on the silent street with only the sound of the waves to disturb the night, she was simply a woman wanting a man, the man who now held her with the warmth and urgency of his kiss.

Involuntarily her arms rose to embrace him, feeling the rough weave of his linen jacket as she pulled him into her. His hand was straying, through her hair, down her milky white neck, playing about her shoulders, his fingers finally invading the delicate barrier created by the boat neck of her dress. As his fingers fluttered about the delicate bones of her neck and chest, Faith was shocked back into reality.

What was she doing? This man threatened everything she believed in, and she was reacting to his

every whim. As the realization of what was happening
dawned on her, Faith drew her arms away from him
and placed them on his chest, shoving him back into
the dashboard of the car.

In one swift movement she was out of the car and
running toward the door of her house, toward safety,
away from his disconcerting presence. In an instant
the door was closed behind her and she leaned against
it, grateful for the darkness of the house, grateful for
the cool sea air that cooled her blood. As she caught
her breath, she sank to the floor and began to giggle.
Slowly at first, then uncontrollably. As she heard the
roar of the car pulling away from her house, the sight
of the fogged car windows came to mind, and she remembered the days in high school when a car was the
only place to explore and challenge a member of the
opposite sex.

It all seemed so funny; they must have looked like
teenagers out on a first date, struggling in the family
car. Her giggle reverberated through the house, and it
seemed like hours before she realized that her face
was also wet with tears and she was still sitting on the
cold, hard floor.

*Oh, I hate him,* she thought sadly. Her mood
abruptly changed to a wistful melancholy as she rose
and made her way to the bedroom where she would
sleep alone in the large bed.

# Chapter Three

Faith sighed with relief as she opened the door to the office. All was quiet, and she was glad that she had decided to go into work earlier than usual. She was in no mood for the secretaries' speculation as she walked briskly through the bullpen where they usually sat, hands poised over their typewriters.

Continuing on, Faith quickly reached her own office, set apart only by the small nameplate beside the frosted glass window. Throwing open the door, she strode inside, flinging her large briefcase onto one of the green chairs as she went. As the heavy leather case fell to the floor, missing its target, she stopped for a second, tensing her shoulders as she heard the thud.

If there were any more problems before the day even started, she felt she'd scream. Bailiff had taken a little walk and had not come home, and her favorite blouse had a stain on it. She seriously considered simply turning around and heading back to her warm bed when Darcy's voice cut through the still air of the old building.

"We're early today." Faith glanced up to see her secretary's smiling face poking through the door. Looking back at her desk, she began to shuffle through the papers she had disregarded the night before.

"Mark should be here any minute," she stated flatly, knowing that he probably wouldn't be in much earlier than nine. Faith felt Darcy hesitate for a minute. She knew the woman was dying to know what had happened the previous evening but hoped that she had made it clear she was in no mood for a discussion. But to her relief, Darcy simply turned and walked away, leaving Faith to work for a solid half hour. Time enough for her to banish her morning peevishness.

"Well, you look as if you're deep in thought. What's up?" Mark MacMillan had entered her office without her hearing him, and she jumped at the sound of his voice. Smiling up at him, hiding her mood, she brushed back her hair.

"Well, good morning," she returned the greeting. "No, not deep in thought, just trying to shake off last night's sleep, what little I had." She shrugged her shoulders and settled back into her large chair as Mark threw an envelope on the desk good-naturedly and took a seat across from her, propping his feet up on the desk.

"You do look a little peaked. What gives?" Faith looked up. She and Mark had been friends for years and dated off and on between assignments. Unfortunately Mark's attachment for her was greater than Faith's for him. She hesitated. Should she tell him about her date last night? Why not? He didn't own her, and as far as she knew, jealousy was not one of his failings.

"It was an interesting evening. I had dinner with Jim Stanten." There, she had said it. Mark simply raised an eyebrow in response, casually urging her on.

"It was the strangest thing. He called out of the blue and asked me to dinner. I thought I might find out something I could use during the trial." The tall, lanky man across from her interlaced his fingers and placed them against his lips.

"And did you?" he asked.

"No, not really. There were one or two surprises, but nothing earth-shattering." She looked Mark straight in the eye, all the while berating herself for the lie. Why hadn't she just told him she had learned nothing and left it at that? Was she subconsciously trying to lead him on, asking him to question her about the night before? Did she really need to talk to someone that badly? But Mark simply continued to stare at her, his expression unreadable. Faith became uncomfortable under his intense gaze. Perhaps he would let her comment and her tone of voice go unnoticed.

The silence stretched before them like the strain of a taut rubber band, but only Faith seemed uncomfortable in the quiet. Picking up the manila folder Mark had tossed on her desk, she released the metal clamps on the back and removed the contents.

"This all you have?" she asked in a professional tone, her eyes lowered as she scanned the papers in her hand.

"I'm afraid so. It doesn't look like much, but it's solid. I checked it out myself."

Faith glanced up at him suddenly as the full implications of Jim Stanten's accusations came back to her. A shadow crossed her brow as she looked at the sandy-haired man, but he was not cognizant of her scrutiny and continued.

"We have depositions from the distributors. One of our own guys infiltrated the ring about six months ago, and when we made the bust, we picked up records of shipments, names of the people who supplied the kids. Got a good stash of pictures, too, but you may want to have a cup of coffee before you go over them...." His warning came too late. Faith had already discovered the pictures and sat mesmerized by the frightened young faces.

Faith lowered the last of the photos onto her desk and looked out the dirty window at the brown air of the city. Sadness descended upon her like quicksand, slowly, methodically engulfing her until she could no longer breathe within its confines. Again and again as she looked out the window, she saw the face of Jim Stanten appearing before her mind's eye. She could see him laughing, talking over dinner. He had been attentive, delightful and charming. But with unrelenting clarity his face became sharper as she now saw him for what he was. He must know what his client had done. How could he in all good conscience defend a man like Bennett? Which, then, was the real Jim Stanten—the one who could make her feel like the most desirable woman on earth or the one who turned a blind eye upon the pain and suffering his clients inflicted? How could she ever tell? Why would she ever want to find out?

Turning back to Mark, who still sat quietly in front of her, she parted her lips as if to speak, but nothing came out. She passed her slender, manicured fingers over her throat as though that slight action would relieve the pressure inside her body.

"I know, Faith; it's hard."

She smiled at him weakly, grateful that he understood. All thoughts of Stanten's accusations left her mind as she looked at the upright agent.

"Listen," he continued, "I've got to go. If you need me, just holler."

Faith nodded her head. It was hard to feel sorry for herself when people like Mark saw this kind of thing day in and day out and were still asked to lead normal lives, still asked to function in a society they knew was ill.

"Thanks, Mark. I'll talk to you later." The voice she had finally found was small and quiet. Faith did not look up as the door shut quietly after Mark's retreat.

For a long while Faith did not move. The phone rang but was picked up by a prearranged signal with Darcy on the third ring. She wasn't even curious as to who might be on the other end. Finally forcing herself to move, she calmly and firmly put her mind into the proper gear to deal with what lay before her.

As though an icy film had formed over her eyes, she picked up the first photo that lay before her and reviewed it clinically. She noted every angle, the age of the children involved; she recognized some of the people with the children from previous investigations and did not fail to add the notation to the others on her long legal note pad. All these things would be useful when they finally came to trial. Later she would review the photos once again. Then she would cry over them, allow every emotion to come into play as she looked at the tiny, pinched faces so that her opening statement might be as forceful as her closing arguments. That was what a woman brought to the courtroom—thought and emotion. That was what allowed her to succeed where others failed, and she utilized every part of her psyche to accomplish her task.

Her eyes lingered over one photo in particular. It was different from the rest, almost artistic in its simplicity. The sadness and suffering that emanated to the viewer was akin to the first time one's eyes rested on the Pietà. The room depicted in the photo was stark white. It was as though the little blond girl stood before a photographer's seamless screen, there were so few shadows, so little definition in the walls. The background was simply a hazy gray. But from some unknown source of light, the little girl's small body was illuminated. Faith guessed the girl could be no more than seven or eight years old, but the dark eyes could have belonged to a woman of thirty, a woman who had seen it all.

It was those eyes that caused Faith to hesitate and then turn the glossy picture over and scan the back. The little girl was Meg Cortland, age ten. That surprised Faith. Usually she guessed the ages of these unfortunate children right on the mark. A series of notations listed the foster homes that Meg had been in, the last one for three years. Three years too long, for it was that home that led the poor little thing into the situation Faith was now trying to rectify.

Clearing her throat, Faith tried to retain her objectivity. This was not the time for emotion; that came later. But no matter how hard she tried, she could not stave off the well of emotions beginning to rise within her. What was it? Anger? Sadness? Care? Longing?

All those things swirled and danced in her mind as she once again perused the features of Meg Cortland. Faith found it difficult to think about children other than as they related to her work, as detached objects of crime. But ever since she was a little girl herself, she had known that she wanted to be a mother and would be a good mother. Now, the years racing on, Faith tried not to think of children in terms of herself, in terms of her ever bearing a child of her own.

But as she looked at Meg, all the longing for a child came back to her. There was something ethereal about the little girl. Perhaps it was simply the photograph, the luck of the shameless photographer who took it that for once in his life he had actually created a picture of worth. Whatever was beginning to possess her unnerved Faith. Disregarding the rest of the photos, she sat back in her chair and continued to stare at the picture for a long time before picking up the phone.

"Darcy," she said quietly into the box, "I want you to get a hold of Mr. MacMillan. Have him call the case worker for Meg Cortland." She listened for a moment as Darcy spoke, then replied. "No, that's spelled with a C. I want to set up a pretrial interview—say, Thursday of next week."Again she listened as Darcy read back the order. Usually Faith would allow a brief prayer of thanks to cross her mind for the likes of Darcy. Not only were they friends, but she was also the most efficient secretary Faith had ever had. Now there was no time for such appraisals. The only thought that persisted in her mind was of Meg Cortland. Suddenly Faith had a premonition that the little girl would play a very important part in the upcoming trial . . . and maybe even in her own life.

It was one o'clock before Faith checked her watch and finally acknowledged the hunger pangs that were plaguing her stomach. With a sigh she rose from her desk, rubbing her tired eyes as she made her way to her office door and threw it open. The entire office was silent. Five minutes more and everyone would be returning to finish off the day's work. If she was going to get any lunch, she had better do it immediately.

Once on the street, Faith looked left and right, trying to decide where the best place to grab a bite to eat would be. She wanted to be someplace with people, so many people she wouldn't have time to think about Jim or Meg or the trial. Turning to her left, she headed toward Olivera Street. The two-block walk did her good, despite the feverish heat.

Faith always felt as though she had stepped back in time as she entered the one-block alley of Olivera Street. It was like being in old California once again. Olivera Street was the first settlement in Los Angeles, and even though the adobe buildings now housed shops and restaurants, the flavor of the original site was still evident. Down the center of the brick street, kiosks were set up displaying the wares of Spanish leather workers, cotton Mexican wedding dresses and traditional Mexican sweets. On either side of the alley, shops and eating establishments displayed colorful piñatas in their doorways, enticing tourist, secretary and executive alike to sample their wares.

Faith strolled about the street absentmindedly, touching a dress here and a leather belt there. Though the mad crush of the street was exactly what she sought, Faith did not really want Mexican food, so when she reached the end of the block, she turned east and made her way through the endless traffic toward Felipes.

Down the ancient stairs and through the double wooden doors Faith went until she stood on the outskirts of the cavernous main room of the restaurant. It seemed that the entire work force of downtown Los Angeles was seated at one of the many long, long picnic tables or standing in lines waiting to be served. Above her, Faith noted the huge chalkboard that hung suspended from thick chains over the heads of the waitresses as they scurried about filling orders, their white winged hats bobbing on their heads. Her attention did not linger long for she always had the same thing. Instead, she scanned the lines of hungry people. Even at one o'clock all six of the lines seemed to wind around the tables and almost to the door. With a shrug of resignation, she chose one and waited until it inched forward and she stood in front of the high glass counter.

Ignoring the display of meats and pickled eggs, she stood on tiptoe and almost yelled her order to the blue-haired woman on the other side. Within five minutes the woman returned with a corned-beef sandwich piled high with meat, a giant kosher pickle and what seemed like a pint of cole slaw. Grabbing the tray, Faith elbowed her way out of the line and started climbing the steps to the second-floor dormitory, where more benches were set up. Mentally patting herself on the back for not spilling her milk, she laid the tray down on the end of one table so that she could sit facing the wall.

Idly she munched on her sandwich, her mind playing about all the things she had to do. Pick up her shoes at the repair shop...start work on her opening statement...compile information on Meg Cortland. Meg Cortland. Such a small key to bring down such a large man, Faith thought involuntarily. Suddenly Faith felt someone behind her and instinctively moved closer to the table so that he might pass. Lost in her thoughts, she never turned to look at the diner.

"Faith?" a deep voice disturbed her; the man had not passed but was still standing there. Tilting her head backward, she looked into the sparkling eyes of Jim Stanten.

*I must be dreaming,* she thought calmly as she once again noted how beautiful his eyes were without his glasses. *The man is really getting to me. I think about the case and he appears.*

"Faith, can I sit down, or are you just going to stare at me for the next ten minutes?" She started as though she had just been awakened by an intruder in her home.

"Of course, if you like," she answered, pulling her thoughts into the present. Faith noted he carried no tray. "Aren't you eating?" she queried, trying to sound matter-of-fact.

"No, I just finished. Look, I do want to apologize for last night. I was out of line." He seemed contrite, and Faith decided to meet him halfway.

"It's okay. If that's what you believe happened on your last case, there's nothing I can do to change your mind. I just don't believe what you told me about Mark, but your apology is accepted anyway." There, she had said it. Quietly, nicely, one lawyer to another, while her body titillated, her nerves danced as he took the seat next to her.

"Oh, I don't mean about MacMillan," he said seriously.

She opened her mouth to protest; he could have been gentleman enough and let that whole subject lie, but he stopped her with a quick motion of his hand.

"I apologize for my juvenile behavior when I took you home last night. I just happen to think that, well, you're a very attractive woman and I'd like to get to know you better. Do you think that's possible?" His expression was sweet, his face devastatingly handsome.

His intent perusal of her was disconcerting, and her mind flew, exploring every avenue of argument that presented itself to refuse him. He was everything she disliked in an attorney, but quite a few things she liked in a man. After all, he hadn't exactly tried to rape her the night before. His actions were the same as any other man's might have been. Hers, on the other hand, were quite unusual, considering her normally restrained nature.

Carefully she answered him, "I think that's possible. As long as we take it slowly, you see—"

"I know. I know about the quiet life you lead. I can't say that I lead the same type of existence, but it might be interesting to see how we mesh away from the courtroom. I already know there's no chance for a truce inside those hallowed walls." He was smiling at her now, small pearly teeth peeking out from under his mustache. "I'm still stinging from that suppression-of-evidence hearing."

Now Faith smiled, too. The professional compliment was almost as pleasing as the way his warm, full lips had felt on hers.

"Well, since you put it that way, I suppose seeing each other now and again won't hurt anything."

"I didn't mean now and again," he said and placed his hand over hers. She felt the quickening of her blood. "I thought we could make it more often than that."

Faith lowered her eyes. She knew instinctively that she would give in to this man, and he could destroy what little faith she still had left in herself as a woman. She could possibly destroy him in the courtroom, but was it a fair trade? Then, as she contemplated his proposition, she became aware that they were no longer having a private conversation. Looking up, Faith's eyes were locked by the contact with Robo Bennett's small, clear blue eyes. She was only vaguely aware of the two large men who flanked Bennett.

Jim had risen to his feet, and Faith almost knocked over her tray as she turned to face the men, the hard wooden bench sending a shot of pain up her spine as she did so.

Even though Faith had never met him in person, there was no denying that it was Bennett who stood before her now in the flesh.

"Aren't you going to introduce us to this lovely lady, Jim?" The man's voice was soft considering the great bulk from which it came.

"Faith Karell, Robert Bennett," Jim said with his usual flair. There was no note of embarrassment, no hesitation, on his part during the introduction. Faith wondered how he could stand there so calmly, knowing how she hated the man. Was it really worth the effort to try and build a personal relationship with Jim when he could so obviously turn the charm on and off like a light?

"So this is Faith Karell. I understand you're going to be trying to put me out of commission for a while, little lady." Bennett's ringed fingers played with his necktie as his eyes turned cold and bored through Faith.

"I'm afraid you heard wrong, Mr. Bennett. I *am* going to put you out of commission and it won't just be for a little while. I intend to make this one stick." Her tone was hard and sure. She was not going to be intimidated by him now. Not when she could still see Meg Cortland's face in her mind. For herself, for Meg and all children like her, Faith was bound and determined to make this man squirm. And if need be, do the same to Jim Stanten.

"Well, that's awfully big talk from a little girl." He

laughed, turning toward his two companions, who smiled grimly along with him. She could not tell whether his tone was threatening. He was a smooth operator.

"Faith has an excellent record in the courtroom, Mr. Bennett," Jim broke in before Faith had a chance to retort. "She's going to be a worthy adversary, but then, so am I." Faith looked at him. It was as though he were trying to protect her, stop her before she said anything she would regret, anything that might bring harm to her.

"Don't you think we ought to be going, Mr. Bennett?" Jim suggested abruptly. The large man looked at the attorney, a hint of surprise playing on his face. His snakelike eyes seemed to weigh all the possibilities open to him. He seemed to be wondering if he should make a scene. But Jim stood his ground under the close scrutiny, never wavering under the man's stare.

"Yeah, I guess you're right." He turned once more to Faith. "Nice to meet you, Miss Karell. See you in court." He hesitated for a moment before he moved away from the table, then turned once more to look at Faith. "Did anyone ever tell you you ought to be in the movies?"

With that, he was gone, followed by his ominous-looking bodyguards, who chuckled, too, as they left the restaurant.

Faith's face burned with embarrassment and anger. She hardly noticed that Jim had lagged behind. Then, as he touched her shoulder, she looked up at him, her lips clenched into a severe, thin line.

"I'm sorry, Faith, I thought he had already left. I'll call you." In an instant he was gone, following his client.

Pushing her tray away, Faith crossed her arms on the table and hung her head, trying to regain her composure. Now, more than ever, she was determined to put Mr. Robert Bennett away for so long that by the time he got out of jail no one would even remember his name.

But Jim... how could he even associate with such a man? After all, he was no fool, he knew the score. Defending Bennett was tantamount to approval of his client's actions. Was he then no more than a wolf in sheep's clothing? And what would she do if he called? How could she even consider the possibility of a man like that touching her? Wanting her? More important was the question of her own burning desire, which seemed to flame rather than wane with the passage of time. It seemed to her that he would have to change a lot before she could ever consider letting him into her life. She would just have to steer clear of him until this whole thing was over. Maybe then she could look at him in a different light... but sadly, she doubted it.

In ten minutes Faith was back in her office. With renewed fervor and dedication she tackled the pile of books and files on her desk. She had to be absolutely prepared to meet her opponents once again in the courtroom. She was determined that not the slightest bit of evidence would be missing from her attempt to rid Los Angeles of a man like Robert Bennett. Thank goodness it was the end of the week. Two whole days at home with her books and briefs, without the normal interruptions of the office, would give her the edge she needed.

Darcy poked her head through the door and addressed Faith, who never looked up from her writing. "I got the number of the place Meg Cortland's been assigned to. Do you want it?"

"Um, hm," Faith acknowledged the question as she flipped through a book with her left hand and picked up a pencil with her right.

"It's the Jackson residence, 555-1839, Mrs. Cornelia. The lady doesn't work and has been on the Foster Care Program for about six years. Good record. The little girl's being well taken care of." Darcy disappeared, and Faith considered the phone number for a minute, wondering if she should wait until the interview Thursday or give Mrs. Jackson a call immediately.

Something inside her drove her to pick up the receiver and dial the number. There was really nothing she could accomplish over the phone, but the need to have some contact, any contact, with the girl seemed overwhelming. The phone rang; one, two, three times. Then a woman answered the phone, her voice slightly nasal.

"Is Mrs. Cornelia Jackson there, please?" Faith queried.

"Speaking," came the curt reply.

"Mrs. Jackson, my name is Faith Karell. I'm the prosecutor on the case against Robert Bennett and I'll be visiting you and Meg next week to discuss her testimony." Faith could feel a shiver of excitement run up her spine as she talked to the woman. She now knew that this little girl was the key to winning the case. She would have to be very careful when she spoke to Meg so that she would not frighten her in any way.

"Yes, Miss Karell, I had a call warning me that you would be contacting us soon. I..." The woman hesitated, as though she wanted to say something she knew she shouldn't.

"Go ahead, Mrs. Jackson. I know this isn't going to be easy." Faith led her on. People like Cornelia Jackson needed to get things off their chests, too, and so often they had no one to share their feelings with.

"Well, to be perfectly frank, Miss Karell, I don't really approve of trying to put Meg on the stand. I don't know if she can take any more."

"Is she psychologically disturbed?" Faith began to take notes.

"Of course she is... but not in the way you mean. Meg is a fine little girl, but right now she's afraid of her own shadow. Do you know what that poor, delicate little thing has been through?" The woman's voice was rising. "Do you know what those people made her do while your system let her go on living there so they could exploit her?"

Faith shrank from the woman's accusations. The system wasn't perfect. How would the caseworker ever know Meg was in trouble if all she saw was a clean, seemingly happy home that housed a middle-class family?

"I understand what you're saying Mrs. Jackson, but my system, as you call it, can only do so much. There are some things that happen to hurt us all, and we try to rectify them when we can, when they are finally brought to light." Faith's voice was calm and soothing as she spoke into the phone. She was looking forward to meeting Mrs. Jackson. The woman's conviction fairly flew over the line that connected them. Thank goodness for people like her. "Does Meg have any real family?" Faith asked.

"No." The woman's voice had dropped in a sigh of resignation. She knew she couldn't fight Faith, but she had at least made a stand. "Meg was abandoned by her father when she was three. Her real mother died a year later. She's been shuttled between foster homes since then."

As the woman spoke, Faith fingered the photograph of the little girl. How could they...everyone... how could they have done this? Their actions were not only against all laws of the United States but against all things in human nature. If there was a true reincarnation of pure evil, then these people had to be part of it. Her heart went out to Meg, and she found herself hoping that perhaps Mrs. Jackson would let her see Meg alone.

"Mrs. Jackson, would you have any objections to my seeing Meg before next Thursday? It's hard to explain, but I really feel the need to get to know her...not just take her deposition for court. Do you think that could be arranged?" The hopeful tone in Faith's voice did not escape the woman.

"I think that would be all right. When would you like to come?"

"Would tomorrow be too soon?" Faith asked.

"You are anxious, Miss Karell. But I suppose that would be all right. Just remember that you're not going to find a bouncing little girl when you get here. Meg Cortland will never know what it's like to be a child, so you might as well be prepared. Good-bye. I'll see you tomorrow." The click on the other end of the line signaled the end of their conversation, and Faith felt lighthearted, almost happy, that her curiosity about Meg Cortland would be satisfied so soon.

Faith sighed as she went back to the work on her desk, knowing that the resolution she had made to work until the desk was clear was a frivolous one. At five-fifteen Faith packed her briefcase for the weekend and quietly closed the door to her office, knowing that tomorrow was going to be an exhausting day.

# Chapter Four

"Hi, Mrs. Gardner," Faith called laconically over the fence to her neighbor as she made her way from the garage to the back door of her home.

Things always went on. She knew that every Friday she would offer the same greeting to the strange old woman who made shell sculptures in her yard, and every Friday she would receive only a terse nod of acknowledgment. It seemed that Mrs. Gardner did not approve of women who worked outside the home but, sooner or later, Faith was going to get her to talk. It was a matter of principle now. She often wondered why the old woman was always out in her garden only on Fridays, rain or shine. But after living at the beach for so many years, Faith thought, maybe Mrs. Gardner had a mind that was as fried as her deeply wrinkled tan skin.

Dismissing any more thoughts of Mrs. Gardner, Faith went about her usual Friday routine. Feed Bailiff, pour a glass of wine, get the mail and collapse on the sofa in the living room.

Fridays were for her and her alone. No work would

be conducted this night. Even she, dedicated old
Faith, needed to walk away from her work every now
and then. She might watch some ludicrous situation-
comedy on TV or settle down, swathed in her biggest
terry robe, for an evening of music and a good racy
novel.

Glancing across the street, she made her way to the
little mailbox, noting that the beaches were still populated with hundreds of sun bathers. It had been a great
day, and she found herself almost envying all those
people who had the free time to enjoy such beautiful
weather. It had been hot, but the fiery edge of the
Southern California sun had softened, leaving only a
lulling warmth.

Grabbing the large handful of mail that had been
forced into the tiny receptacle, Faith sighed and
moved over the little brick walk that led back to the
house. Bailiff was munching happily away at his dinner as Faith retrieved the wineglass she had set down
on the coffee table, kicked off her shoes and settled
back into the deep cushions of the sofa to peruse her
mail. Bills and more bills. Charge accounts, water,
electricity...ah, a letter from a friend in the Peace
Corps. Faith set the letter aside for future reading
when she knew she would be thoroughly relaxed and
her mind clear.

The Drug King was having a sale, and there was a
catalogue from one of the neighborhood dress shops
that specialized in polyester pull-on fashions...defi-
nitely the junk pile. Suddenly she stopped. Her eye
was caught by a simple black-and-white flier, the face
of a foreign child on the front, wide-eyed and seem-

ingly frightened. Holding up the piece of paper, she noted it was a plea for money to adopt a child by mail in one of the Third World countries. Ten dollars would feed, clothe and educate such a child, it said.

As Faith looked at the picture of the little black-haired girl, the image was slowly replaced with the face of Meg Cortland, and Faith rubbed her eyes, attempting to bring the real face back in focus. Why didn't these do-gooders take a look at home before they went around trying to save other children? Adopt a child…sure…and what do you give them? Money? Of course. But there was never the chance to hold that child or talk to it, love it. Somehow Faith felt she could throw ten dollars into the gutter in one of the poorer parts of Los Angeles and it would do more good than sending it to the Save the Children campaign. Who ever knew if you really helped the child they photographed for their fliers anyway? No one was really sure that the help arrived. Meg Cortland again floated to the top of her mind. She shook her head, trying to dispel the image. This was her night, and she wanted to leave behind everything that had happened during the week.

As she raised the glass of wine to her lips and tossed the piece of paper into the junk-mail pile, the phone rang, startling her and making her spill a drop or two of the liquid on her silk blouse.

"Damn," she said under her breath, unsure as to whether she was condemning the wine on her blouse or the person on the other end of the phone who dared disturb her during her one night without work. Putting the long-stemmed glass on the table, she rose and moved toward the small alcove that sheltered the telephone.

"Hello," she demanded into the receiver, daring the person on the other end to respond cheerily.

"Hi." It was Mark MacMillan who greeted her. "Listen, I'm going to be a little late tonight. I've got to check on a few things at the office. I'll pick you up about eight o'clock." The initial peevishness of her tone melted into one of utter confusion when she answered him.

"Mark, I..." she began, trying to cover her irritation.

"Don't tell me you forgot, babe." There it was again, that awful term of endearment.

"I'm afraid I did. What are you talking about?" she asked, allowing the slip to go uncorrected.

"Tonight is the party at Jenkins, VonDerlieth and Jenkins to announce the new partners. How could you forget the biggest wingding of the year?" Now it was Mark's turn to sound a tad upset. As well he should, since they had made the date ages ago. How could she have forgotten?

"Well, I guess it just slipped my mind. You know I'm not much for those kind of things. Why don't you go ahead? I think I'll just stay in tonight, okay?" Crossing her fingers, she hoped he would quickly agree and let her go back to her wine.

"Faith, what is the matter with you? Ever since we started getting close to a trial date, you really have changed. Don't you want to see me anymore? Is that it?" She hated confrontations like this. It wasn't as though they had been going together. He was just a casual date for her, someone to pass the time with. Maybe she hadn't made that clear. Her thoughts were cut short as he continued, not waiting for an answer.

"Look, we've been planning this thing for a month, and I've really been looking forward to it. Can't you make an exception and come with me?" His voice had taken on a soft, pleading tone, one which made Faith's hair stand on end. She didn't like it when he turned the tables like that. Why did men have to play these games better than women?

"All right, eight will be fine," she said with a note of resignation that Mark either ignored or missed completely.

"Great, you know half the legal population of Los Angeles will be there. We might pick up some great tidbits of information." His instant joviality was annoying, and Faith cut the conversation short, saying good-bye and replacing the receiver with a sigh.

Hell, she thought to herself as she stood, unmoving, in the center of the room, this thing is supposed to be formal. She really would have to do a little shopping; it looked as if her social life might be picking up.

Jim Stanten loomed in her mind as she headed toward the bedroom for a short nap and then a warm bath. He would be there, she knew. A glittering affair such as this would not be the same without the infamous young defender. She wondered how she would react to him when they met that night. She also found herself pondering the question of whom he would be with.

Faith had congratulated herself on putting the man out of her mind during the afternoon, but now his image was before her again, larger than life in her mind. He was a chameleon—there was no other way to describe him—sensitive one moment, cool the next as he catered to his unsavory client. She couldn't help but think that some of the underhanded methods his clients used in their businesses had to rub off on Jim. It would all be so simple if people just treated each other with respect. Then there would be no need for her or Jim, nor would there be any people like Robert Bennett or his victims.

Throwing her blouse and skirt toward the large basket she used as a hamper, Faith decided not to try and anticipate a confrontation that might never happen. She was going to put any thoughts of Jim Stanten out of her head. Given his life-style and his obvious lack of taste in clients, there was no chance that he could ever mean anything to her other than being a thorn in her professional side... unfortunately.

Faith raised her arms above her head as her tub filled in the bathroom and stretched her body to its limits, attempting to exercise some life into her tired bones. A few sit-ups and toe-touches later, she was feeling a bit more lively and was actually beginning to look forward to her evening out.

Maybe Darcy had been right all along. She did need to get out more. She would try to look at Mark in a different light, too.

Faith knew she was not meant to be a solitary figure, nor was she destined for life in the fast lane. But the men she met, day in and day out, never seemed to be able to supply the balanced type of relationship she craved. Perhaps if she just gave Mark a chance, she would discover that he was the one who could fulfill her need. After all, they thought alike, worked toward the same goal.

Dismissing the thoughts immediately, she stepped into the warm bath and washed away the worries of the day. As the summer sky began to darken, Faith reluctantly left her tub and buffed her skin until it tingled. Slowly she creamed her body, lingering over the soft flesh of her breasts as she once again succumbed to the unbidden memories of Jim's lips on hers, his fingers playing about her neck.

"Stop it, Faith," she commanded herself, speaking her thoughts aloud. "He's not for you. Just face it!"

Quickly she donned her robe, covering her lithe body and removing any temptation to relive the short but sweet memories she had of her night with her legal adversary.

"Hi, Bailiff," Faith addressed the cat as she moved into the bedroom and picked up the old, round alarm clock by the bed. "Now I just want to sleep for an hour or so. When this goes off, if I don't hear it, you jump right up and wake me, okay?" She smiled at the cat, unaware after all these years that she spoke to the animal as though it were a human being, her confidant, her friend.

Lying down on top of the slick coverlet, since the cool ocean breeze had not come to ease the heat of the day, Faith closed her eyes and was lulled into sleep by the softly fading light that came through her window. But her rest was not to be a calm one. As she teetered on the edge of deep sleep, still clinging to consciousness, faces flashed through her dreamlike state. Bodiless phantasms cavorted about in her brain, each topped with the head of those who now ruled her existence: Jim, Meg, Bennett, Mark. All flew about with little regard for her desire to escape into the darkness of sleep. Even in her bed she was not safe from their constant harassment. She was alone and they were as one body, each interacting with the other. She was the one on the outside whom they tormented. Then the visions of her dream seemed to be fading into one, each beckoned and was taken by the most powerful of the ghosts until finally only one face, the face of Jim Stanten, filled her dream. As she watched, his noncommital face slowly brightened with a warm and wonderful smile that, rather than comforting her, tore at her soul as she fought the invitation it seemed to offer.

With a sudden start she was awake, shaking, disturbed by the dream. Enough, she decided. Let me be. With that she rose from the bed and flipped on the stereo, allowing the brash sounds of the rock station to saturate her mind. Letting her body move to the beat, she rocked back and forth near the bed, attempting to let the music encompass her. Turning it even louder, she walked into the kitchen and brewed a cup of tea. Putting the pot on the back burner, Faith once again retraced her steps to the bedroom, turned off the alarm that would have rung a second later and seated herself at the dressing table. The music was beginning to infiltrate her hazy, sleep-laced mind, and the tea almost made her look forward to the evening's festivities.

With unusual care Faith attended to her hair and

make-up. A bit of blush and black mascara, clear gloss for her lips and her make-up was complete.

Pulling her hair back into a high pony tail, she secured it with an exquisite comb of curved silver overlaid with electric-green cloisonné. A black velvet skirt, its ruffle adding length that was no longer strictly fashionable, was paired with her stiletto-heeled boots and a matching chiffon blouse. It was an ensemble of understated simplicity. The monochromatic coupling of pieces caused her to look taller, slenderer than any human body should be. Clasping a silver bracelet to her left wrist, Faith stood before her mirror, creamy skin contrasting with the understatement of her dress. Subconsciously she acknowledged the sultry woman who stood imprisoned in the mirror, but as she turned away, no longer reminded that she was that woman, the image was dismissed from her mind and she went to wait for Mark to call for her.

That wait was not long. By the time Faith had rinsed out her teacup and the pot, replaced both in their rightful places and refilled Bailiff's water dish, he was at her door.

"Ready to go?" he greeted her casually.

"Sure," Faith answered, picking up the purse she had placed near the door. Flipping out the light and locking the door, she turned to Mark and they made their way to the car, chatting casually until he opened the door and she slipped into the seat.

They sat in comfortable silence, as friends and colleagues sometimes do, each wondering what the night would bring. But as she exhausted her imaginings, Faith looked at Mark once again as she shifted in the uncomfortable plastic seat of his government-issue car. Again she saw with disappointment that Mark looked somewhat discombobulated: his tie too wide, his shirt unstarched, his polyester pants paired with his one good wool blazer. She knew his attire shouldn't bother her, but for some reason she was simply uncomfortable sitting there in the nondescript car with the nondescript man. Was it too much to ask to admire the man she was involved with for everything he was?

Of course, Mark was a physically handsome man, with light hair and blue eyes, a tanned and muscular body. But when he dressed he seemed to detract from his natural good looks as though he was ashamed of himself. Or did he actually think his choice of clothing enhanced his physical appearance? Why did it bother her so much? She quickly drove the unkind thoughts from her mind and tried to pay attention to what Mark was saying.

"... don't you worry about a thing. We're going to nail those bastards if it's the last thing we do. Just stick with me. I know how to get them." What did he mean? Was she reading something into his comment that wasn't there? Perhaps now was the time to ask him about Jim Stanten's accusations. But wouldn't a question like that immediately give credence to the statements made against Mark? She hesitated, then answered.

"I'm sure we'll do just fine. But let's not talk about the case now. Let's just have a good time tonight." She couldn't do it, couldn't ask him. Was it that she was afraid it might be true? After all, Mark had such a highly refined sense of justice that he might have stretched a truth a little, but perjury? Never! She put it from her mind.

"Well, that sounds a lot better to me, too. I've really been looking forward to this for a long time. We haven't seen each other socially for ages." His hand covered hers that lay in her lap, and she felt herself cringe from his touch. Faith had promised to give him a chance, but there was something that just didn't click when he touched her. She wished she could explain it, wished she could change it. She would have to give him a chance, but why couldn't he be a little more subtle?

"Maybe tonight," he went on, "we can share a nightcap together, if you know what I mean." He looked at her from the corner of his eye and smiled.

"We'll talk about that later," she said testily and then quickly softened her tone. "It may be a late evening." Faith hoped he would get the hint.

"Sure, whatever you say." The smile had not left his face nor his hand her lap. "Here we are," he continued as she shifted again in her seat away from him.

Faith looked up as the car dipped into the cavernous opening to the parking lot under the steel-and-glass high-rise. Noting the prices posted on the lot, she clicked her tongue.

"I can still remember when parking in Los Angeles was free," she said almost to herself. "Now they want ten dollars a day. It's outrageous."

"I know. Life just isn't fair, but we all do what we have to to rectify it, don't we?" His voice seemed to carry a hidden meaning and Faith was disturbed.

"What do you mean 'what we have to'?" she queried as he expertly pulled the car into a small space between two pilings.

"Just what I said. Sometimes you bend the rules a little. Did you know that when I flash my credentials, I can get out of a speeding ticket or park in a place like this for free?" He chuckled to himself, proud of the privileges his status as an FBI agent afforded him.

"Mark," she admonished, "you don't do that?" Faith was shocked into immobility.

"Of course, don't you?" He looked at her quizzically, his surprise genuine.

"No, I can't say that I do." Her stony reply curtailed any further information and Mark got out of the car. Faith didn't wait for him to reach her side, and she was already standing in the damp concrete chamber by the time he reached her door.

Taking her arm in silence, he led her to the elevator banks that would whisk them to the lobby to transfer to another elevator and yet another before they would reach the party on the fiftieth floor. It was in the lobby as they waited for the elevator that Mark put his hands on her shoulders and spun her toward him. She was surprised at the force of his actions, and it plainly showed on her face.

"Sorry," he stated simply. "I didn't think I had turned you that hard." Her black eyes burned into his; she could feel her anger rising both at his misuse of his position and casually offhanded bragging about it.

"What's wrong with you?" he asked. "Are you angry about my little transgression with my identifica-

tion? Faith, it's no big deal." He was almost pleading
with her to understand and her mind raced. It really
wasn't anything so terrible, really. Such a small thing.
She shouldn't be upset. It was just like professional
courtesy with doctors.

"I'm sorry. I'm not really upset. I'm just surprised.
You of all people. I thought we were alike . . . ." Her
soft voice trailed off.

"But we are, Faith; that's why we make such a
good team. We both want to put the bad guys away.
Don't let this upset you. It's no big deal. In fact I think
that you're probably the only one who doesn't do it."

"You're probably right. I'm sorry. I promise not to
ruin the evening," she said contritely, though in her
heart she still did not approve and wondered what
other transgressions he was guilty of.

They both turned as the chrome-and-bronze elevator door opened, allowing them to enter. As the doors
closed behind them, Mark leaned down and kissed
her lightly on the lips.

"All forgiven?" he asked, smiling down at her.

"Of course," she said, attempting to return his
grin, but she wished he hadn't done that. Somehow
she wasn't really looking forward to the party anymore; she wished she was home with one of her pa-
perbacks and a glass of wine. It just wasn't any good
between them on a personal level. Where was the fire
her mother and friends always talked about? The
answer came to her quickly, piercing her consciousness like a finely honed sword—Jim Stanten, that's
where the fire lay.

In a matter of minutes they had transferred once

again and were transported to the floor that housed the offices of Jenkins, VonDerlieth and Jenkins. The doors slid open one last time, and they were ushered into the stunning lobby of the law firm.

There were people everywhere. Women were dressed in the most beautiful designer dresses, both stately and funky. There were a number of gentlemen in tuxedos, but most had opted for the classic dark suit. One or two were attempting to make a statement by wearing jeans, but Faith was sure they were not the elite of the legal field in Los Angeles, but probably some of the new breed who practiced their law in the back buildings of Santa Monica and the outer reaches of L.A. proper.

Mark gripped her elbow firmly as he guided her through the glittering mass of people. The pressure on her arm stopped for a moment as they thanked a waiter who offered champagne and caviar. Then, once again, they were off to tour the offices and congratulate the new partners.

Faith had recognized a number of federal and state judges as they wound through the array of beautiful bodies. The conversations seemed to be as bright and brash as the surroundings were understated and sophisticated. Faith was amused as she looked around. All the trappings of a movie set surrounded them. It was as though the decorator had read all the clichés about law and chosen the decorations of the office to fit.

Everywhere there were antiques, heavy wooden rolltop desks, ancient library stands and frothy ferns. Oriental rugs covered the floors in shades of bloodred and midnight blue; impressive books and ledgers were dusted and displayed in the lobby area, and Faith wondered if the covers bound anything other than empty pages. She was almost sure they were nothing more than shams, accessories picked for their color rather than their content. While she was trying to imagine herself in such surroundings playing lawyer in the opulent offices, Mark addressed her.

"Faith, I just saw Ray Gianturco. I think I better go over and say hello. Do you want to come?" She just shook her head above the din of the conversations and picked another piece of quiche off a passing plate, unwilling to shout back to him.

"Okay. I really think it's a good idea to keep on his right side, if you know what I mean? You be okay here alone?" Once again she nodded, swallowing the last delicious mouthful of cheesy pie.

As she watched him go, she almost felt a relief. She so much more enjoyed watching the race about her as people made contacts and broke contracts, all the while keeping a mask of sincerity and gaiety firmly in place.

Finally tiring of the polite conversation she was forced to make as she was caught by a person here and there whom she barely knew, Faith escaped from the lobby area and roamed about the seemingly endless offices, listening to the sound of the party grow dimmer and dimmer. Like a child exploring a new play area, she peeked into offices, admiring the furniture and artwork she found in each one. At the end of the hall, she could hardly hear anything, and she snuck into the office of the senior partner Mr. Jenkins, hoping to find a place to put her feet up and enjoy the solitude and the excellent champagne.

She was not disappointed when she entered the bastion of the great defense lawyer. Obviously no expense had been spared by the decorator. The mahogany-covered walls shone in the dim light that emanated from the small, brass, green-shaded lamp on the desk. Mr. Jenkins's diplomas, earned so many years ago, were tastefully displayed behind his enormous desk. The other walls boasted their burdens in an understated manner; oil paintings, modern and classic, hung in discreet placement on them and Faith noted that all were originals. Quietly she moved about the room, her footsteps silenced by the thick pile of the ruby rug.

"Good evening." Faith was startled out of her perusal by the sound of a quiet voice that emanated from the burgundy leather chair behind the desk turned to face the wall. Slowly the chair rotated and Faith was aware of the figure that sat huddled in it, only the glint of a crystal glass visible in the dim light.

"I'm so sorry. I hope you don't mind my snooping..." If this was Jenkins, she would die.

"No, not at all. In fact I was hoping to get you alone in a dark room." She moved closer; the voice was familiar and the scent of the sea was evident as she moved toward the desk.

"You!" Her surprise was evident as Jim Stanten reached over and turned the desk light twice, the bulb in the lamp glowing brighter with each turn, illuminating his handsome face.

He leaned back once more, enjoying the shocked look on her face, and smiled at her, a winning, warm smile. His eyes casually appraised her, taking in the rich cut of her clothing and the shine of her boots. Finally his eyes came to rest on her face as his eyes looked frankly into hers.

"What are you doing here?" she gasped, trying to recover her wits.

"Probably the same thing you are. Looking for a little peace and quiet."

"I didn't think you would want to escape. There's enough glitter out there to satisfy the most hardened connoisseur of that sort of thing," she said testily, embarrassed that he had found her wandering here and disturbed her so suddenly. He had not even given her a warning. How long had he been watching her, she wondered.

"I'm afraid you do me an injustice. I'm not all flash, you know." He motioned to a chair and Faith, for some unknown reason, obeyed his command and sat stiffly on the velvet-covered seat. He towered over her as he launched into a vivacious speech.

"There are a few things you should know about me," he went on. "For instance, I love cats and I hate pomp. I like to roam around art galleries even though my apartment is filled with glass and chrome. I hate my glasses but need them for reading." Faith could stand it no longer and interrupted his litany.

"Why would I want to know those things?" she challenged him. "I already know all I care to about you. You make your living by helping people evade the law, people who hurt others and use them."

"What I do for a living doesn't necessarily mean that I live my own life the way they live theirs. Didn't it ever occur to you that there is also some good in helping people who are accused as well as assisting the accuser?" He was obviously unruffled by her angry attitude.

"What possible good could there be?" He was doing it again. Leading her into a conversation she had no desire to partake in. Faith could not understand her never-ending curiosity about the man. And curious she was, no matter how hard she tried to deny it.

"You know, not all of my clients are like Bennett. He is the exception rather than the rule. Some of them, the white-collar criminals, if you like, are really just desperate people playing at money games and losing. They're confused, stripped of power, ostracized from their friends; they need someone to listen who can understand them. Once they have committed a crime, it's usually their last. They are ashamed, broken human beings. Don't you think those people are allowed a defense?" She looked at him closely. He was obviously sincere in his belief that anyone should have someone to defend them properly. She really couldn't deny the truth in his argument. That was the way the system was supposed to work.

"But you play ball to win. If you don't believe you're doing the right thing when you defend people like Bennett, why do you do it?" She had to know and know immediately, for she could feel his presence beginning to affect her. The fluttering in her stomach was real and in a moment if would move up to her heart and her mind.

"Faith, it's my job," he said gently. "Unfortunately, most of the human race does not have the same highly refined sense of justice that you do. We are not willing to give up everything for what is always right. We take the good with the bad. That's how life usually works." Although he looked at her, he seemed not to see her as he continued, "Oh, we don't mind discussing it and philosophizing about what's right and wrong, but we don't have the guts to face it head on like you do. You really are quite a special person." His eyes had wandered and he was now considering the beautiful crystal glass he held in his strong hand.

"I love the law." He glanced up at her once again. "Please don't scoff," he begged when he saw her face break into a wry smile of disbelief. "I do love the law: its intricacies, its imbalances, its striving to be always better. I'm proud to be a part of it, but to me it is a talent, something I do very well, not some kind of religious calling. Can you understand that?" The tone he had adopted was not one of a frivolous man trying to placate an outraged woman. He had simply stated his philosophy and he was proud of it. The quiet strength that his attitude exuded did not escape Faith, and she sat considering the man in front of her.

She had to admire him. He made no excuses for his existence or his way of life. But then, didn't he have every right to be proud of a job done well just as she did?

"Yes," she said quietly, "I can. But that doesn't mean I agree with it."

"No need to," he answered, rising from the chair, empty glass still in hand. "That's what makes the world turn. People should have different opinions, different ways of life. After all, without people like me where would you be? You wouldn't have anyone to fight against." He stood over her, his hands wrapped around the bowl of the glass and she tilted her face up questioningly.

His right hand released the glass and strayed to her hair, hovering above it for an instant and then lightly touching the cloisonné comb. She held her breath. Even this slight gesture caused her to shiver with expectation.

"Pretty," he said almost reverently, and then, slowly, he bent one knee to kneel before her, putting the glass down on the deep carpeting. Neither noticed that it had fallen over as his hands rested on the arms of the chair, and he leaned ever closer to her as though time had stopped and they had an eternity to linger over the kiss that was softly shared.

Closing her heavily lashed eyes against the light, Faith allowed herself to drown in the delicious sensation his mouth was creating. The pressure was light but forceful as he explored her lips, moving about, trying to find the perfect meeting place. He did not open his mouth to search hers, only chastely moved his head slightly now and again to allow his passion to be known and not feared as befitted a tentative new lover.

"Faith, don't condemn me now. Give me a chance," he whispered when his lips finally left hers and he had buried his head in the soft cleft of her shoulder. "I won't change who I am, but I will please you. I will, if you let me."

A shuddering sigh escaped from her lips as she relaxed against him, pleased to remember how good it could feel to have a man so close, pleased that she could accept his advances without once thinking about the courtroom and her responsibilities. Her hand rose to touch his thick hair and run her fingers down his neck to the tip of his perfectly starched shirt.

Raising his eyes to look into hers, Jim remained kneeling as though he were paying homage to a saint when suddenly the overhead lights were flipped on, startling them out of their common entrancement.

"Well, are we having fun?" The strident voice of a stunning blonde broke the mood, and Jim retreated casually from his place on the floor, stood up and faced the woman.

"Sandy," he said cheerily, "how good of you to come look for me." A slightly sarcastic undertone was evident in Jim's voice as he greeted the visitor.

Faith could feel her skin burning, blushing like a school girl caught by an irate parent in her first kiss. She also rose, trying to think of something to say. Obviously the woman had come with Jim. How awful she must feel finding them there like that. The woman moved toward them, her walk sultry.

"This is Faith Karell. Faith, Sandy Druid." The two women exchanged nods, one terse, the other shy.

"It's getting late," Sandy said, ignoring Faith as she played with the lapels on Jim's tuxedo. Faith suddenly felt very small and very plain. The woman was unbelievable. She was tall and willowy, endowed with a curvaceous body. Her dress was long and silvery, low cut in back and front. When she walked toward Jim, she exuded the kind of raw sensuality that Faith could never hope to possess.

But to her surprise Jim dismissed the woman. "Why don't you go and find your purse, and I'll meet you in the lobby." With a sullen look the woman turned on her heel, glancing icily once more in Faith's direction.

"Of course, darling, if you insist. It really is time we go home." The way Sandy spoke the word *home*, Faith wondered if they lived together. As if reading her mind, Jim moved toward her and took her in his arms.

"No, she isn't someone special. She just likes to think she is," he said softly. "Perhaps we could continue this discussion later?"

She nodded, confused as to her feelings, only knowing that she would see him again, must see him again. With a light kiss on her forehead, Jim departed, following the blond woman into the great mass of people who still lingered about the office. Unconsciously, Faith bent down and picked up the glass Jim had laid on the carpet. Holding it to her breast, she went in search of Mark. She, too, wanted to go home.

# *Chapter Five*

The ride home from the party seemed inordinately long. Mark had definitely enjoyed himself, and his driving showed the effects of the champagne. More than once Faith had offered to drive, but he had shooed her away, insisting that he was fine and there was no need to worry.

But she was worried. Mark had become a different person, loud and obnoxious, and Faith was beginning to wonder why she had ever gone out with him in the first place. They had known each other for so long, but sitting beside him, she realized she didn't know him at all. Drink did strange things to people, things she didn't like, especially in friends.

"Well, here we are, little lady," Mark was drawling like Ed McMahon on "The Tonight Show," and Faith was grateful that they had reached her house in one piece. "That wasn't so bad, now, was it?" He had slumped back in his seat and had turned blurred, vacant eyes upon her. Faith's only answer was a deep, disheartening sigh as she put her hand on the door latch.

As she started to open the heavy door, he clapped a strong hand on her arm. "No need for that. I haven't forgotten that I'm a gentleman." His voice was almost unintelligible and his tone was bellicose.

"It's all right Mark. I can make it in by myself." Faith kept her voice modulated, trying to calm him down.

"I insist.... I won't hear of it." Faith was surprised by the alacrity of his movements as he got out of the car and moved around the front end, bumping into the fender and taking a moment out to apologize to the car. She couldn't help but smile at the scene before her. If only he knew how silly he looked: big, strong FBI agent reduced to a blubbering idiot by a few glasses of champagne.

Then her door was opened and a waving hand reached in and grabbed her arm. "Permit me," he said with exaggerated grace.

"Thanks, but I think you had better permit me," she retorted wryly and put her arm about his waist, stumbling as he leaned into her. "I think you better have a night cap before you leave."

"How'd you know that's exactly what I need?" His words spewed forth in one exasperating string so that Faith could hardly understand him.

"I mean the kind that's strong and hot and black." she replied, knowing that she was destroying the little fun he had left in him.

She fumbled with her keys as Mark slumped against the side of the house. Finally the door was open and a lamp illuminated as she helped him into the living room.

"Boy, you smell good," Mark mumbled into her hair as his head bobbed against her. "You smell so good I could just eat you up." His hand moved up and down her shoulder as they moved toward the couch.

"Mark," Faith said, shaking away his lips, "cut it out." Finally she deposited him on the sofa with a warning. "Now you stay there and I'll be back in a minute with a nice cup of coffee."

"Whatever you say, darling." His hands fell to his side as he sank into the cushions. Faith could feel his bleary eyes watching her as she left the room.

Rummaging through the cabinets, she finally found a teaspoonful of instant coffee left in a jar. As she popped a cup of water into the microwave oven to heat, she found herself wondering if Jim had ever been in the position Mark was in now. She really couldn't imagine him out of control of his senses.

The bell on the oven signaled that the water was heated, and she dismissed thoughts of Jim for the moment. Three minutes later she reentered the living room balancing the coffee, a glass of water, and a bottle of aspirin. Mark was stretched out on the sofa, his eyes closed, but as she approached they flew open and a lopsided smile came to his face.

"My angel of mercy," he said, raising himself with difficulty.

"Believe me, Mark, I'm no angel. Now take these." She held out two aspirin and the glass of water. Mark complied, almost choking on the little tablets. "Now the coffee," she went on and reached over him to retrieve the steaming cup, but before her hand reached the china it was caught in his.

"I don't need any coffee, Faith," he said, causing her to look directly in his eyes. "I just need a little loving." His hand moved hers to his shoulder and clumsily he tried to move closer to her over the tops of the deep cushions.

"You need coffee, Mark," Faith answered, her patience waning. "You need coffee and you need to go home. Now drink it." Her tone was commanding and Mark returned her look with an angry one.

"Don't tell me what to do," Mark retorted, taking the cup and sipping despite his objections. Faith sighed and started to rise but immediately Mark's hand shot up and grasped her again at the elbow.

"Mark, what do you think you're doing?" Now she was mad. She was tired and in no mood for this little game of cat and mouse.

"Come on, Faith, it'll be great to get to know each other a whole lot better," he mumbled as his grip became viselike and he pulled her back onto the couch. His bleary eyes were open and his face was coming closer to hers.

"Mark, damn it. If you're well enough for this kind of joke, you're well enough to go home." Faith hissed the words at him, wrenching her arm free. "Don't be an idiot. This isn't funny anymore," she cried as she moved away from him quickly, putting enough distance between them so that he could not possibly grab her one more time.

"I didn't mean it to be funny. It never has been for me." Mark's voice was gaining strength as he became angry at her rejection. "All this time we worked together and went out and you never gave me a chance.

Well, I want a chance now." Faith was stunned as she watched him. Where was the guy whose praises she had been singing for so long? This wasn't the Mark MacMillan she knew.

"Damn you, Mark. Why did you have to do this?" Now her whole body was shaking, reverberating first with fear, then with relief. "I thought we were friends!"

"We are, Faith," Mark said, hanging his head, "I just want it to be so much more. You should know how I feel. Hell, we're together almost every day; you should know." His speech was slurred again as he let his head fall into his hands. Faith felt no sympathy for him.

"I don't care what you wanted. You would have been out of here ten minutes ago if I could have moved you. What in the hell makes you think I'd want to take you to my bed?" Her voice was reaching a point of hysteria as the full implications of his actions sank into her mind.

"Well, I just figured it was about time." His sheepish look did nothing to abate her anger, and she lashed out at him once again.

"How dare you figure anything of the sort! When I want someone to be my lover, I choose who and when. Do you understand that?" Faith's anger was beyond control as she looked at the pale, disheveled man. Who did he think he was? She had never given him any reason to think that he could take such liberties.

"All right, all right . . . no need to get so upset." His casual manner was once again evident. It was as though he had just stepped on her toe rather than having made such a loutish, rude pass. Faith seethed with fury and sat silently staring at him until she felt she could control herself.

"Get out of here, Mark. Just get out and go home. I'll see you on Monday." Her voice was weary now, and she wished he would just leave so she could collect herself alone. At that moment she wished she would never have to lay eyes on him again.

"Listen," he said, approaching her slowly. "It wouldn't have been so bad, would it? I mean our getting together?"

"It would have been awful," she lashed back, stopping him in his tracks. "Don't you have the first idea of what a woman wants or needs? How dare you come in here and treat me like that!"

For some reason her statement made him angrier than Faith ever thought was possible, and he came quickly to her side and stood, staring down at her from what seemed like a great height.

"Like a man, you mean? Just because I don't sweet-talk you like Stanten? Just because I don't wear those fancy clothes and drive that fancy car." The shocked look on her face seemed to amuse him. "You didn't think I knew where you were the whole night? 'Little Miss Right' is getting down with the biggest slob they ever let take the bar." Mark's tone was cruel and biting, and Faith crumbled under it, trying to control the tears of rage that were springing to her eyes.

"So I figure if you're good enough for a louse like him, you're good enough for a lowly agent like me. Now, let's cut this out and get to it." He was sneering at her now, and the fear she had successfully quelled returned.

"You're still drunk," she said evenly, knowing that she had to control herself, show no sign of the fear that overtook her. "Now just turn around and get out of here." She punched the words hard and they finally seemed to register in his mind.

Mark passed his hands over his eyes and sighed a soul-wrenching sigh. His shoulders slumped and he turned to go. It was as though he were Jekyll and Hyde, and Faith didn't know what to make of his behavior. Would he turn on her again or leave?

"Go home, Mark," she said again, this time with more force, hoping that since he was reacting to her commands, she should reiterate them, not give him time to change his mind again.

Mark looked down at her for a long time, and Faith held her breath, afraid he would reach for her. Instead he threw his head back and sighed rather than spoke the words. "Faith, I'm sorry. I am so sorry."

His head fell to his chest and he was gone. She listened intently until she heard the front door close behind him. Then, jumping up from the floor where she still sat, she ran to the door and locked it with the dead bolt.

Slowly she made her way through the house to the bedroom, not stopping to clean up the coffee and water. Not bothering to turn on the light, Faith undressed in the darkened bedroom, leaving her clothes wherever they dropped. Turning back the covers, she crawled into the inviting bed.

The pillows whispered softly as they gave way

under the light weight of her head. For a long time she lay awake. Confusion overcame her. Had she been making the wrong assumptions? Was it Jim Stanten who was the one she could rely on and trust? Everything was upside-down. Mark, the one person who truly shared her desire to rectify the injustices in the world, had just attempted to perpetrate the greatest injustice on her. Jim, who defended those wrongs everyday of his life, had treated her like a lady, like a woman of worth, a person to be respected.

She had no idea when sleep finally overtook her, mercifully releasing her from her anxious thoughts. But sleep she did, heavily though, for when the morning light woke her at six, she did not feel rested. Her body ached as though she had been tense and ready for another intrusion on her privacy, on her psyche.

The long, hot shower she took seemed to ease away some of the tension, but she still was unnerved by Mark's advances of the night before. For some reason, she longed to call Jim Stanten, simply to hear his voice. But what would she tell him? That the man he already thought had perjured himself had also proved to be personally unethical, disappointing Faith beyond belief. It sounded so ludicrous, so totally ridiculous when she went over it in her mind that she wouldn't have breathed a word of it to anyone, much less Jim. Besides, she still wasn't sure if she should, or could, trust him.

Dönning her well-worn jeans and a crisply starched work shirt that showed flecks of ancient paint, Faith wandered about the house and into the garden. Settling herself on the little brick wall that surrounded the sapling in her yard, she looked up into the sky. It was clear and bright . . . so good, offering its warmth to everyone, yet she felt as though the sun shone just for her. God's medicine for an aching soul. She closed her eyes, offering her naked face to its healing rays. Solitude was wonderful, strengthening, but she really didn't want it to be this way forever. She wanted to share everything—her work, her home—with someone who would love those things as much as she did.

Jim Stanten surely could understand her work, but empathize with her conviction? There was no answer, not yet. Mark understood all right, she thought scornfully, but look where her trust and sharing had gotten her.

Squinting down at her watch, she noted that there were another three hours ahead of her before she could make the long drive to Long Beach and Meg Cortland. Ah well, she thought, standing and stretching her arms above her head as though she could touch the sun, might as well get some work done.

Fifteen minutes later Faith's coffee table was buried under papers and books as she delved into her work. Checking and rechecking references, looking at the pictures now and again to refresh her memory, revived her indignation. All thoughts of Jim and Mark were put out of her mind as she fell into the arms of her first love—the law.

The phone had rung every hour on the hour, and now, as she prepared to walk out the door, it was jangling again. Faith looked at it, weighing whether or not she should pick it up. If it was Mark, she didn't want to talk to him. She couldn't even think of him without the anger beginning again. If it were anyone else . . . well, it didn't really matter. She made a mental note to invest in an answering machine at the earliest possible date and walked through the door locking it behind her.

There was something absolutely exhilarating about driving on the labyrinthine freeways of Los Angeles on a Saturday. The traffic moved along briskly, and everywhere cars were carrying surfboards and chattering teenagers, as mothers headed toward the beach with their laughing children. One felt as though one were flying and distance meant nothing on a beautiful Saturday in a little Volkswagen heading for the sleepy little town of Long Beach.

Orange Avenue, Cherry Avenue, Signal Hill turnoffs all whizzed past Faith until she reached Bellflower Boulevard, where she finally steered the crotchety little car onto the off ramp and onto the wide boulevard heading toward Park Estates and the little girl who would help her nail Bennett.

She drove down the tree-lined streets, watching the houses go by slowly, each one of them set far back from the avenues atop beautifully manicured lawns. At one time Park Estates was the only bastion of wealth in the small town. Safely nestled behind a high, long wall, the community had been populated by the lawyers and doctors of the area who had taken great care in building their homes.

Each was unique, large and rambling in the true California style. Now the nouveaux riches had begun to make inroads into the sanctified neighborhood. No longer were old, distinguished people the only ones out for a walk on the quiet streets. Now the well-dressed children of the young entrepreneurial set played football and rode their bicycles through the winding avenues. Faith smiled. It was good to see such life breathed into a neighborhood of beauty and refinement. These children were definitely privileged. She hoped they appreciated their good fortune.

Finally Faith found Los Flores Avenue and made a hard turn down the short street, which ended in a cul-de-sac. She peered out the open window, mentally counting off the street numbers as she went. In a moment she had stopped in front of a beige, ranch-style home. Three children were sitting quietly on the sloping emerald lawn underneath an olive tree. Two preteen boys and one little girl looked up as Faith approached.

"Hi," she said cheerily when she was within hearing distance. "Is this the Jackson home?"

"Yep." The one who answered seemed to be the oldest boy. Certainly he was no more than ten or twelve but already he looked as if he was in high school. Kids sure were growing up fast these days. Faith thought.

"I'm looking for Mrs. Jackson. Is she here?" Her smile failed to get a friendly reaction, and the older boy simply pointed toward the house.

"Go around the back to the garden," he finally called, even though she was already headed up the driveway to the front door.

Changing her stride, Faith walked all the way to a small gate in the back of the house. She had never seen a drive so long in a private neighborhood such as this. Opening the gate, she entered a small garden area where at least fifty plants were in different stages of growth, some almost ready for planting. There were trash cans and a tool shed to her right and everything was spotlessly clean, even the trash barrels. Ahead of her was another gate, which she quickly unlatched and walked through.

Certainly she must be in Disneyland, she thought as she surveyed the land around her. The lawn, the flowers, the enormous swimming pool were absolutely perfect in every detail. The garden was alive with color, and the only sound was that of a bluebird calling to its lost love.

Looking down the long lawn and past the sparkling pool, Faith saw Mrs. Jackson stretched out on a canary-yellow lounge chair, a large straw sun hat covering her face. Faith started toward her and just as she was about to call so that she would not frighten the woman, she saw the little girl.

Meg Cortland sat on the redwood deck just behind the older woman. Her head was lowered and her hair fell over her face. Meg's hands rested, unmoving, in the space between her crossed legs. She didn't move a muscle even when Faith hailed them.

"Mrs. Jackson?" she said loud enough for her voice to carry in the quiet yard. The woman looked up and smiled gently. Faith was sure that Mrs. Jackson never smiled any other way; she seemed to have the grace that comes with practice. Her husband was a doctor, and she had probably spent many hard years scrounging to make ends meet. Now that they did have leisure time and money, the woman probably harbored fears of losing it all again. She was careful, hiding her feelings behind a mask of subtlety.

"You must be Faith Karell." She had risen, her hand extended as she moved toward Faith. "I hope you didn't have any trouble finding the house."

"No, not at all. I appreciate your allowing me to come on such short notice. I promise I won't be long." Faith smiled at the woman and thought she saw a flickering in her eyes, a lowering of her guard, but only for an instant.

"Take as long as you like," she answered. "As you can see, Meg is a very quiet child. It may take you a while to get her to open up ... if she ever does." With that Mrs. Jackson walked away, her svelte, jump-suited figure disappearing through the sliding glass doors off the patio. Faith heard her speak in Spanish to someone inside and figured it was the maid. As the two women's voices faded, Faith turned her attention to the little girl who still had not moved from her seat.

Quietly Faith moved toward the lounge that Mrs. Jackson had occupied only minutes earlier. Lowering herself gently on the yellow plastic, she carefully laid her large canvas purse down and removed her sunglasses. Sighing to gather courage, Faith finally spoke.

"Meg." Still the little girl did not look up. Why hadn't she paid more attention in psychology class? Faith thought to herself.

"Meg," she tried again. "My name is Faith. I'm here to help you if you'll let me. Do you understand?" Receiving no answer Faith plunged ahead, figuring that a steady stream of chatter might bring the little girl out of her stupor.

"I work for the government. I'm a lawyer. Do you know what that is? I help put bad people away so that they don't do bad things anymore...as they did to you. Do you think you could tell me about what they made you do? It sure would help because I have a very hard job and I can't do it alone. I need you to help me. You're the only one who can."

Faith was becoming exasperated. The little heap of humanity at her feet was so different from the surreal picture she had been looking at for the last twenty-four hours. There was nothing unearthly about this little tyke. There was only a heavy sadness around her, a burden so great that it bowed her little shoulders until she could not even raise them anymore.

"Meg, guess what? I brought you something." Faith reached into her purse and pulled out a roll of Lifesavers. Heck, it worked in the commercials, and now anything was worth a try.

"Here." She held the roll out to the little girl, waving it slowly under the waterfall of hair, unsure as to where her eyes were. Just when she was ready to give up, one of the little hands moved and captured the candy, opening it and popping one into her hidden mouth and retreating back to the safety of her lap.

Faith smiled. "Now," she said happily, "isn't that better?" She was making progress. The head nodded up and down.

"You know, Meg," Faith said cautiously, "I have a cat. Do you like cats?" Slowly the hair fell away as Meg lifted her face to meet Faith's gaze, and she nodded her head up and down, her soulful eyes gazing into Faith's. This was the little girl in the picture. How they had ravished her. The depths of her eyes were unreadable, holding the memories of things not even an adult should possess.

"Meg, can you talk to me?" Faith inquired gently, trying not to frighten the little girl. "If you don't want to talk about what's happened to you, we can talk about anything you like." Her tone was hopeful, but there was no conscious effort to speak on Meg's part.

For a long time Faith sat and carried on a one-sided conversation there in the bright sunlight, nestled in the soothing garden. The little girl's eyes followed her every time she moved her head or gestured with her hands. It was as though she were waiting for Faith to lower the boom. She could imagine how the girl felt. After all, people like Bennett used the same tactics: sweet talk, then force. No wonder Meg was wary.

At some time during their conversation, Faith couldn't remember when, the Mexican maid had appeared, stealing out to the backyard to leave a glass of iced tea for Faith and a Coke for Meg. Now, exhausted, Faith sat sipping the cool, refreshing liquid as she stared into Meg Cortland's eyes. The girl did not waver under the gaze; instead it was Faith who finally had to turn away.

Mrs. Jackson appeared at her side none too soon and Faith was as relieved as though the cavalry had just arrived.

"Not having much luck are you, Miss Karell?" the woman asked, looking at the little girl.

"No, I'm afraid not. Poor little thing, she must be terrified of any new face that comes into her life."

They moved off, away from Meg who once again lowered her head.

"Isn't there any way to reach her?" The pain in Faith was more than evident to the older woman.

"Miss Karell..." Cornelia Jackson began.

"Please call me Faith."

"Thank you, Faith," she resumed. "We've been taking care of Meg for over three weeks. Every morning she comes out here and sits in that corner, hangs her head and doesn't say a word. We haven't heard her speak yet, and we have really tried to bring her out. Even the children are depressed. This isn't the first unfortunate child we've had in this house, and usually the other kids in the neighborhood bring them out in a matter of days." The woman seemed genuinely concerned and Faith was touched that this cool, calm matron of Long Beach society cared so much.

"It's obvious you have put a lot of time and effort into Meg," Faith complimented her. "Can you think of anything that might help? Anything at all? She seems like such a dear child."

Mrs. Jackson hesitated and then turned to face Faith straight on. "The only thing I can think of is a permanent home with people who love her and won't run away at the first sign of a problem. Unfortunately we can't keep her. I've wanted to keep every child who ever came through this house, but there are certain things that are just out of one's control."

Faith found herself wondering what Dr. Jackson was like. Was he the one who objected to adopting the children Cornelia so obviously cared for? Faith dismissed the thought as unfair. How could anyone be expected to adopt every unwanted child that passed through his home? It was just great that people like the Jacksons were foster parents.

Somehow, though, Faith felt that Mrs. Jackson was challenging her personally with her words, but the hidden meaning escaped her. "I understand. I imagine it would take a whole lot of constant love to get through to her."

How sad, how utterly unfair, life was. "Well," Faith continued after a moment's silence, "I better be going. I'd still like to keep my appointment next Thursday, if that's all right with you. I'd like to put Meg on the stand, but she's going to have to open up a whole lot more in order for me to do that. Would you have any objections to my taking her out for the day?" Faith asked hopefully.

"Of course not. It might be the best thing for her." The woman smiled her enigmatic smile once more and Faith turned to cross the yard.

As she walked down the long drive, Faith began to think of ways she could pull the little girl out of her depression and fear. Then from behind her, she heard footsteps . . . small feet running in rubber-soled shoes. Faith turned and looked behind her.

There was Meg, running as fast as her skinny legs could take her. In an instant she stood before Faith, her head bowed, her hands clasped in front of her. Faith didn't speak, waiting to see what would happen next. Then, as though she were a wind-up doll, Meg spoke. Her words were even and devoid of any inflection.

"You're pretty." Two words, two wonderful words!

Faith bent her knees and put her hand on the little girl's shoulder, tilting her head to the side so that she could peer under the mass of soft hair.

"You're pretty too, Meg," she said softly. "I'll see you in a few days, okay?"

Rising to her feet, Faith turned and made her way to the car. She fought the urge to look back, not wanting to do anything to break the happy mood that the two words had bestowed upon her. Once she had started the car and shifted into first gear, she ventured to glance up one more time, but Meg Cortland was nowhere to be seen.

"Just as well," she sighed. "Can't hope for too much too early." With joy Faith began to sing at the top of her lungs along with the tune that blared out of the radio to fill the tiny car.

As the little red Volkswagen flew along the San Diego Freeway, Faith frivolously gave in to a whim and turned off the drive into the Carson Shopping Mall. Why not allow myself a little fun? she thought.

For three hours Faith amused herself by peeking into shops, trying on clothes and snacking on junk food. Finally she decided it was time to head home. She carried two bags. One held a long, red silky negligee, a purchase she had no idea why she made. In the other was a crisp white dress dancing with lavender flowers. The perfect thing for a little girl, the perfect dress to bring Meg Cortland out of herself, out of her silence. Both were ridiculous purchases, but Faith could not help herself. After all, she was a lady alone, so why not splurge every now and again? But somewhere, deep in her mind, Faith knew that the two garments she carried were symbolic of the change in her life. Subtle changes in which both Jim Stanten and Meg Cortland played a bit part.

When she finally reached her house, she thought again, consciously this time, of the clothing. What had made her purchase those things? She had no one to wear the negligee for... or did she? Could it be that she wished to dress the way she thought Jim Stanten would like his women? No, that was a silly thought. Faith knew she would never change for anyone. And the dress for Meg? She had seen hundreds of children like her throughout her career. Why was this one so special? What kind of web was this little girl spinning around her?

Carefully folding the dress and the gown back into their bags, Faith also packed away any further thought of Meg Cortland and headed back to the dining-room table where her work awaited her.

At midnight she had fixed herself a cup of tea; at one o'clock she had refilled the cup. Glancing at her watch, she saw that the time was coming on 2:00 A.M. Stretching herself out over the pile of books and papers, Faith allowed herself a moment to close her eyes as her head nestled on her arms. She really knew she should be thinking about going to bed, but sometimes, when she was on a roll, she worried that she would lose her train of thought. Sighing she returned to a sitting position and once again began to search for a case that, so far, had eluded her.

She stopped flipping the pages of her casebook for a moment and tilted her head—had she heard a knock on the door? There it was again. Who would be on her doorstep at this time of night? Rising slowly from her chair, she approached the door with apprehension.

"Yes, who is it?" she called cautiously through the heavy wood.

"It's a Greek bearing gifts," the cheerful voice on the other side said. Faith instantly recognized the tone. Opening the door, hand on hip, she faced Jim Stanten. As she flipped on the porch light and looked at him, she broke into a fit of delighted laughter.

There he stood on her doorstep at two o'clock in the morning. In his arms he carried two bottles of wine and numerous small, white boxes from which steam was escaping, sending the smell of Chinese food wafting through the air.

"Well, aren't you going to ask me in?" he asked in mock embarrassment.

"Of course," she answered, finally regaining her composure, hiding the last of her laughter behind her hand. "What are you doing here at this time of night?"

"Well, would you believe I was just in the neighborhood?" he ventured as he laid his burden on the coffee table, spreading the boxes out so that they covered the entire glass top.

"Nope," she answered, slowly closing the door and walking toward him.

"Actually I've been trying to get you on the phone all day," he said, smiling at her. "When I couldn't, I decided to spend a decadent evening at the Ginger Man in Beverly Hills. After all, if I couldn't visit you, I thought I might find some foxy lady to spend the evening with." He shrugged his shoulders, the hint of a roguish smile playing about his lips.

"Well," he continued, attempting now to look serious, "do you know there wasn't one foxy lady to be had at the Ginger Man? Believe me, I looked. Then I decided to go for a drive and where do you think I ended up? Right here. I saw your light on and decided you might be hungry and, *voilà*, Chinese food and wine!" Faith stood before him looking into his eager, boyishly handsome face and could feel her heart melting, touched by his thoughtfulness.

"Well," she said as though she were thinking deeply, trying to hide the emotions that were welling in her, "I guess the only thing to do now is... get some plates and dig in!"

"That's more like it. I'll help." In moments they were seated on the floor of the living room eating the savory food he had brought as though they were starving. All thought of work flew from her mind as they discussed everything from cats to politics over the first bottle of wine. Over the second, after the dishes had been cleared away and Jim had stretched himself out on the sofa, they talked of other things, quietly and intimately.

"Who are you really?" he asked from his comfortable lounge. "You're a beautiful, vibrant woman who becomes a wild cat when faced with a challenge in the courtroom and a shy little girl when faced with the thought of romance. Who are you, Faith Karell?" His voice was soft and low as befitted the small hours before dawn.

She looked at him. How could she answer? So much made up her psyche: the years traveling abroad with her family, living in luxurious penthouses, her sisters' failed marriages. Then there was Meg. The little presence who was becoming more and more important to her with each passing minute. How could she answer him?

When she didn't and simply sat silently at his feet, he continued, "I mean look at you. A beautiful, balmy Saturday night and here you sit with your law books. Is that any way for a woman like you to live?"

"I think it is," she answered slowly, trying to choose her words carefully. "I haven't done a very good job in the romance department. I don't go out very much anymore." She looked at him for a response. For some reason she was embarrassed by what she thought was a failure in her life.

"I know" was all he said. She saw again the handsome features relax into a noncommittal mask as he waited for her to continue. Taking a deep breath, Faith went on.

"And I always had everything given to me. That seemed wrong somehow. When I was maybe sixteen, I realized that it just wasn't the right way to live. So I thought I would do something for people who didn't have it as easy as I did." He was still silent, his only movement a sad, sweet, half smile about his lips.

"I guess that's about all," she said, unsure of what else he wanted to hear from her.

"Is it? Or are you running away? Or do you simply not know how to balance your life? Do you feel so guilty for everything, that you have to immerse yourself in this fight for justice every moment of your waking existence?" He really wanted to know, but she just didn't know how to explain any more than she already had. Faith felt almost naked there in the gray light under his caring perusal.

"I don't know, Jim. I really don't. I guess maybe no one ever paid enough attention to me to help me find out who I really am. But that doesn't mean that I'm hiding behind my profession. I really believe in what I'm doing." Imperceptible lines had scratched themselves into her delicate, creamy forehead as she answered him. Her concentration was complete as she seemed to force herself to think about his questions. Her confusion was evident as the words poured out of her.

"I know you do," he said quietly. "It's part of what makes you so special. It's part of why I can't seem to stay away from you."

Faith watched him closely. It would be easy to fall in love with him as a private person. If only they could stay exactly where they were for the next ten years, it would be wonderful. But she knew that was impossible.

"Jim, I find you terribly attractive," she began, hoping she could explain her feelings to him properly. "You're really a very nice person. You should get a new press agent, you know." Faith smiled sadly at her small joke. "But you and I are different. I can just imagine your life-style, judging by the monstrous car you drive. It's the epitome of show-off rich." He looked hurt and she quickly added, "Oh, I don't mean that as an insult. I just mean that it's different from the way I live." She was trying desperately to make up for her poor choice of words but didn't feel she was doing a very good job of it until he smiled at her.

"I'll say," he answered, glancing about the room, perusing the antiques and expensive knickknacks scattered about the old house, "but why does that mean we can't have a relationship? After all, doesn't something like this deserve a chance? You can't deny the attraction. Considering your love for the law, it seems that there might be some emotion left for loving someone...like me." He did argue his case very well, and Faith smiled at him, a dazzling smile she seldom used anymore.

"That's better," Jim said suddenly sitting up and throwing his legs over the side of the sofa and onto the floor. Setting his glass down on the table, he moved and joined her on the floor, resting his weight on one hand while the other reached over and tilted her chin up, allowing him to look into her delicate oval face.

"Faith, just give me a chance, please." Suddenly, images of Mark MacMillan shot through her mind and she stiffened momentarily, remembering his horrible behavior of the night before. Then she relaxed. In front of her sat a kind man, someone who was offering to work with her, someone who ignited a fire in her body and mind the likes of which she had never experienced. Why not give it a chance? She could only hurt herself...but then she had been hurt before and survived.

With a soulful sadness, she returned his searching look and whispered, "Okay...a chance." When the words were said, Faith suddenly felt relief sweep through her body. With the admission of her feelings, she suddenly felt free, wonderfully alive.

Moving his hand from her chin, Jim captured her head, grasping the wealth of dark, luxurious hair between his fingers, and pulled her slowly to him, kissing her with a softness matched only by the silky sands that lay quietly outside her door to be caressed by the ever-present touch of the sea.

# Chapter Six

"Good morning," Faith said sultrily, the sleep still tingeing her voice as she rolled over on the big bed and spoke into the phone, which had awakened her only three hours after she and Jim had parted.

"Good morning to you, too. How did you know it would be me?" he asked, chuckling into the receiver.

"Just had a hunch," she answered, then hesitated before she continued. "I had a wonderful time last night. I hope you did."

"Better than I ever dreamed possible. Now I know that you've only had a few hours sleep, but I thought we could pick up some breakfast before you felt the need to tie yourself down to your books again. How about it?" Faith felt the now familiar and welcome thrill begin to rise inside her as she spoke to Jim Stanten. Even over the phone he seemed to have some hold on her that she never thought could be possible with any man.

"You promise you won't try to pry any secrets out of me?" she teased.

"Would I do that? Even we shysters have a code of

ethics," he retorted quickly. That was another thing
she liked about him, he was quick to answer and always knew the right thing to say, the right mood in
which to say it. More and more Faith was convinced
that the Jim Stanten she knew, was getting to know
better, was the real one . . . not some fake who would
go to great lengths to win a case.

"All right. Now that I have your word as a gentleman, how fast can you get here?" Did she sound too
excited? Should she tone it down a bit? What the
heck, she might as well enjoy herself. Who knew what
the next few days would bring?

"Why, Miss Karell, I thought you were a liberated
woman. Isn't it your turn to pick me up?" Faith was
not fooled by his mocking tone and challenged him
immediately.

"I'm afraid they wouldn't let my car into your
neighborhood. Now, are you going to come get me or
not?" In the back of her mind, Faith hoped he
wouldn't. She was curious about where he lived, what
kind of personal objects he liked to have around him,
but she couldn't back down now.

"Well, I'll tell you. I will if you insist. But there's a
little place up here that I thought you might enjoy,
and it would save time if you drove and met me. That
way you can get back to work all the sooner." Had
anyone else said that to her, Faith might have been
upset, but coming from Jim the plan seemed ex-
tremely sensible.

"Okay, I'll be up in about an hour. Give me your
address and watch for a car that looks as if it should be
taken away by a wrecker." Grabbing the pad and pen-

cil, she took down the address he gave and hung up. Very ritzy, she decided as she looked at the piece of paper.

With a groan Faith sprung herself out of bed and looked at the clock. Eight o'clock! This was ridiculous. She'd have to work double time today if she was going to be ready for the jury selection in the morning. Deciding not to worry about it just then, Faith headed for the shower and bathed quickly. Tying the straps of her dress as she went to the kitchen, Faith peeked outside and, noting it seemed to be a beautiful, clement day, let Bailiff out as she left the house and got into the car.

The drive was pleasant. At that hour of a Sunday morning hardly anyone was awake in Los Angeles, much less driving. She reached the outskirts of Westwood in twenty minutes and, as usual, enjoyed the sight of the sleepy little college town. Last night she was sure almost every UCLA student had been roaming around looking at the little boutiques or waiting in one of the long lines of the many movie theaters. Some years ago Westwood had usurped Hollywood's status as the area in which to see first run movies. It was a cute little town nestled there between Santa Monica, Beverly Hills and Century City, but Faith had found it a little sad that Hollywood was no longer the glamour capital of the world. She turned onto Sunset Boulevard, shrugging off the thoughts of Hollywood, and found the high-rise building bearing the address Jim had given her.

It was lovely, not quite her taste, but lovely nonetheless. The building reached gracefully and symmetrically to the sky; thirty stories she guessed. Balconies jutted out into the clear sky, eight to every floor. She found a parking space on the street and thanked her lucky stars that she drove a small car. When Faith finally stood in front of the gigantic glass doors, she searched the many names of the listing and finally found Jim's. Pressing the button, she waited and waited. Finally there was an answer through the small security intercom.

"You're five minutes early" came Jim's voice through the mechanical box.

"Sorry. If you're not ready, I'll just camp on your doorstep," she retorted, enjoying the exchange.

"No, it wouldn't look good for the neighborhood. You might be picked up for vagrancy. You know we have a lot of jumpy rich folks in this building," he said happily. A grating buzz erupted from the small box, almost drowning out his last words, and Faith opened the door, heading directly to the elevators without hesitation.

He threw open the door before she had crossed even half of the long hall and peeked out. Seeing her, he lounged casually against the door until she finally stood before him for a moment and then whisked past him into the apartment without a word.

"I'm impressed," she said, trying not to sound so when he finally joined her inside the apartment. "You have good taste."

Indeed he did, she thought to herself as she quickly looked about the living room. A sleek, modern pearl-gray sofa and love seat surrounded a round chrome and beveled-glass coffee table of immense proportions. Above the fireplace mantel he had shadowboxed three Indonesian shadow puppets, the only items that gave the room color...but just enough color. Everything was understated, masculine but not overly so. She hated men who insisted on heavy oak furniture scattered all over the house. She found herself wondering what the bedroom looked like, but instead of verbalizing her question, she moved about toward the kitchen, which was also decorated in the greatest of contemporary taste. Shining brass pots hung from a rack in the center of the room, the walls sported navy wallpaper with a tiny white fleur-de-lis pattern, giving the spacious kitchen a feeling of perpetual cleanliness.

Then she saw it. Eggs, bacon, cheese, all were laid out by the stove. Beautiful French white china and gleaming silver were piled neatly by the food. Slowly she turned to face Jim who had moved to block the door behind her. She motioned toward the food and china, asking a silent question.

"Well," he began sheepishly, "I told you I knew a great place for breakfast...I just didn't say where." Jim's expression was hesitant, waiting to see if it was fury or amusement he was in for. Faith stood quietly looking at him, her hands akimbo on her hips. Finally she spoke, slowly and emphatically.

"All I can say, Mr. Stanten," she said, "is that it had better be good!"

The smile she graced him with illuminated her face, and Jim moved toward her, gently wrapping his hands around her waist. Faith could almost hear her heart beating as his face came closer to hers. She was aware of every nuance of him: his strong, smooth jaw; just the hint of a beard hovering on his chin. Crazily she found herself wondering what it would be like to kiss him if he had a beard instead of his well-cared-for mustache. For she did want to kiss him. Oh, how she longed to have his lips on hers, have him hold her as he had done the night before. But, like the night before, she was concerned that it would go too far. Concerned, but not afraid. Concerned because she wanted him so badly and it had been so long since she had made love to a man. Would she remember how to be a woman? How to be gentle and caring and kind? Not a lawyer looking for the right or wrong of things?

Before she could answer her questions, his lips were almost on hers, hovering just above hers so that she could feel his warm breath. Then, he spoke quietly, before his hungry mouth engulfed hers. "Now, do you really want to eat breakfast or would you like to break another kind of fast?"

Faith's eyes widened slightly, then she relaxed and they crinkled into a softer smile as the world began whirling about her. His lips searched hers tentatively at first. Then they moved frantically, joyously, gently, over her face, his hands still lightly holding her waist. Faith's head fell back, her long hair cascading over her shoulders as she reveled in the feelings that had for so long been so foreign.

Her blood was warm, bubbling just below the boiling point, coursing through her veins, beginning to pound close to the surface. Her eyes fluttered shut, then open again just for a glimpse of his beautiful copper-colored skin, which nuzzled and caressed her cheeks.

Suddenly she could control herself no longer and returned his passionate affections with all the physical force her heart had felt for so long but had been afraid to admit. Her hungry mouth explored his jaw, nipped the small cavern below his ear, nuzzled the strong length of his neck as his hands tightened, then moved from her waist.

A small gasp of sheer delight escaped her lips as his strong arms surrounded her, held her, crushed her to him. She could barely breathe as they became closer than close.

"Faith." His hoarse whisper was like a warm current. Welcome and wonderful in the chilly ocean of aloneness. For so long she had stood on her own. For so long she had wished for someone to love, someone to want, someone to bring her to the zenith of existence. Without this she was only half.

The world was whirling about her as his kisses suddenly stopped, then started again. This time carefully, gently as though he suddenly realized that there was no need to rush. His entire mouth slowly explored hers as though through that one action alone he might possess her. Then slowly he took her hands in his and moved them behind her so that she stood as his sweet captive.

Jim Stanten's eyes bore into those of Faith Karell, asking a question he dare not speak for fear of driving her away by the sheer verbalization of his desires. Seeing no resistance, he twirled her under his arm and slowly led her through the living room and opened the door to his bedroom, all the while holding her tightly about her slim shoulders, kissing her hair and brushing his cheek to hers.

Faith didn't even notice her surroundings as the furniture seemed to melt into a vacuous space, leaving only the king-size bed waiting for them. In one swift movement he had drawn the curtains, leaving her for only an instant. The room, however, seemed to light as the sparks of passion danced between them there in the darkened room. Her breath came short as he once again rejoined her, running his hands over her milky-white shoulders, loosening the hair-thin straps of her dress so that they fell to her sides, pulling the top of her dress down just enough to reveal the heaving mounds of her breasts.

Moments later his square-tip fingers followed the line of her dress, tracing the invisible line of demarcation on her chest, tentatively questioning, asking her permission to continue the hunt for the treasure he so desperately sought. Her only answer was an almost imperceptible sway toward him, and he responded to her wishes.

The sound of the zipper of her dress coursing down her back created an audio aphrodisiac, and Faith could stand it no longer. Raising her arms, she captured his neck and pulled his face toward her with a motion that bespoke of the sharp edge of her torment. In answer, his hands slipped into the loosened dress and held her naked back; the gentle pressure he exerted on her warm, excited skin signaled to her that there was no need for haste, and she relaxed into his arms, enjoying the feel of his hands as they explored her from neck to panty line, lingering gently at the fine lace of her lingerie, then pulling back the elastic and delving gently into the mysterious beyond.

Faith watched him as he stood above her. Then slowly he reached down and slipped her dress from her body as though he were handling the finest of silks. She found herself amazingly alert and wondering at the almost reverent expression on his face. Certainly he had seen many women before prostrate before him, waiting for the culmination of their wordless communication. Yet for that instant, that minute in all of time, he was hers and hers alone and she cared for nothing else.

As his hands moved to idly unbutton his shirt and remove his tight jeans, Faith closed her eyes against his inflaming gaze, trying to hide her insistent urging, wanting to wait for each delicious sensation and not anticipate even the slightest touch. Then he was there, beside her, his hands teasing about her breasts, moving down and sending piercing tracks of desire through her as he cupped the gentle swell of her stomach. She could hold back no longer; his scent filling the room, his symbol of torment pressing into her shapely thighs drove her to the pinnacle of excitement and desire. In a moment she was upon him, reveling in the simultaneous contact of every inch of her body with his as her mouth crushed down on his. The kiss, now returned with the same seething passion, seemed endless. In a flicker of time, Jim was in her, filling her with all the emotions and physical satisfaction that the poets termed love. Love. Yes, her mind cried out, *my love, my love, take me, hold me.* Then in a filling, swelling fit of rapture, they collapsed together, held by the delightful glitter of perspiration that covered them both and sparkled in the whisper-thin shafts of light that danced through the cracks of the drapes.

They lay together for an hour, neither speaking. Now and then, one or the other would succumb to the overwhelming urge to feel once more, discover once more those hidden recesses that people hold so dear, and Faith would snuggle ever deeper into the light cover of down on which her head rested and was supremely happy.

"Now, scrambled or fried. Answer me or you have no choice," Jim called from the kitchen as Faith set the table for breakfast, clad only in his shirt. She was so content. Never before had it been so difficult for her to leave a bed, but Jim had gently reminded her of the work waiting back at her house and she finally relented. Now they moved about in separate rooms but were still bound by the memory of the last two hours.

"I told you, I don't care," she yelled back cheerily.

"Indecisiveness will get you nowhere, counselor. It's a bad habit." He had come to the doorway only long enough to shake a wooden spoon at her before disappearing into the steaming kitchen.

Faith smiled at him as he turned away and finally decided. "Scrambled if you don't mind. And I would prefer not to have you tell me my job. Why, I'm the most decisive person I know."

Jim reappeared, this time carrying two heaping plates filled with eggs, bacon and croissants. He set them down and they took their seats and tasted the food before he spoke.

"Then, if you're so decisive, tell me, what have you decided about me?" he asked seriously.

"I've decided you better not let anyone find out about your soft side or you're dead in the courtroom." She smiled at him teasingly but his face remained impassive.

"I'm not kidding, Faith." She looked at him, not knowing what to say, how to react. He was serious. One afternoon of lovemaking and he wanted a commitment. But then, if she were to be honest with herself, so did she.

"I don't know," she said finally. "You and I live so differently. I just don't know." Her eyes lowered and she pretended to complete attention to the breakfast before her, but he would not let her be.

"No, we don't... not really. It's just the outside trappings that are different. Easy to change. Faith I...." Was he going to say he loved her? She held her breath, waiting.

"I...." He seemed to change his mind and continued in another direction, "I think we could make it work. We need time, I know. I promise I won't push you into anything; just, please, give me a chance."

"All right," came her soft reply, "all right, but first let's see how the trial goes. You may never want to see me again after that battle."

"Or vice versa," he said with confidence.

The mood had lightened considerably by the time Faith was dressed and ready to leave. It seemed as though they could not take their eyes off one another, and reluctantly they exchanged one more long, lingering kiss like high school kids as they leaned against the side of her car.

"Now promise," she demanded lightly, "no phone calls, no interruptions, nothing. I've got work to do and I don't want to be reminded of your existence until tomorrow morning at nine o'clock when we meet on the battlefield."

"Okay I promise," he answered, holding her close, "but don't expect that to hold for the duration of this trial. I don't think I could stand it."

"Neither could I," she admitted sweetly, holding him tighter, enjoying him for one minute longer.

Faith fidgeted with her pencil as Jim once again questioned a prospective juror regarding her knowledge of Robert Bennett. Jim was good, and the selection was taking too long for Faith's taste, far too long. She was blocked at almost every turn. The housewives and mothers she sought so desperately to put on the panel had been methodically disqualified...this one was married to a criminal lawyer, that one spent too much time working as a volunteer with abused children. All of them had some reason Jim could attack to show that they would be prejudiced against his client. Judge Hardison looked bored and the court reporter appeared noncommittal as her fingers flew over her machine. It appeared that only Faith and Jim were totally engrossed in the battle that had been raging for three hours now.

She glanced over at Mark. He had lounged back in his hard, straight-backed chair and looked sloppy— hardly the pulled-together impression the prosecution

wanted to give. She kicked him under the table, and
he sat up, adjusting his tie as he did so, smiling a small
smile at her, a smile Faith did not return. Perhaps he
felt bad about Friday night, but that was no excuse for
his behavior. Liquor was no excuse for acting like a
spoiled teenager. Deep in her heart now she did
wonder about Mark. She had to ask him about Jim's
accusations, had to get that cleared up. There were too
many things on her mind, and that was one that
would alleviate some of the pressure, if she could only
get an answer from him. She would deal with his lack
of personal responsibility after she heard him deny
Jim's charges of professional irresponsibility.

She turned her attention back to the courtroom as
Judge Hardison addressed her. She would have to
stop this daydreaming, although it would be difficult
with the two men who took up most of her life sitting
in such proximity to her.

"Miss Karell," the judge demanded peevishly, "do
you have any questions for this lady?"

"No, Your Honor." She rose slightly from her
chair, pencil in hand. "She is acceptable to the prosecution."

"Acceptable to the defense," Jim chimed in. Once
again, Faith could almost feel the tone of his voice
caressing her as though he spoke to her alone.

"Mrs. Jones," the judge addressed the chunky
woman who sat uncomfortably in the small witness
box, "you are acceptable to both counsels. Thank
you. You may step down now." Judge Hardison
turned back to the courtroom as the woman nervously moved her rock-hard body from the chair,

visibly relieved that she was no longer the center of attention.

"Mr. Clerk," the man on the bench continued, oblivious of the woman's departure, "you may call the next venireman."

The slight, old man's hand reached into the small box that sat atop his table below the judge's raised platform and withdrew a small slip of paper. Faith watched with anticipation as he silently read the name to himself, then made his way slowly to the small door behind him, opened it and whispered the name of the next prospective juror into the room.

Faith smiled wryly to herself as she saw a small, gray-haired woman emerge from behind the door. Watching carefully, Faith assessed the woman called Mrs. O'Hara as she was sworn in and settled herself daintily in the chair, her hands folded neatly in her lap, her eyes turned up toward the man in the black robe.

"Mrs. O'Hara," the judge began kindly, "do you understand that you are a candidate for juror within the federal court system?"

"Yes, Your Honor," the woman replied almost reverently.

"And can you follow the instructions of this court?" he asked again.

"Of course, Your Honor. I always follow instructions of the law," the woman answered a little indignantly.

"I'm sure you do, ma'am. It's just a standard question," the judge went on, easing the woman's mind. Faith watched closely, nodding to herself as the judge continued to ask Mrs. O'Hara the standard questions that would establish her willingness to serve on the jury. In a few moments the preliminaries were over and Judge Hardison looked toward Jim Stanten.

"Mr. Stanten." Judge Hardison gave his approval for the voir dire to begin again. Jim rose gracefully from his chair and approached the podium, papers in one hand, the other moving up and putting his glasses over his clear, innocent-looking eyes.

"Good morning, Mrs. O'Hara," Jim said, smiling at her. "I'd like to ask you a few questions also, if you don't mind?" For the tenth time Faith listened to Jim's nerve-easing introduction.

"Of course, sir," the little woman answered with only the touch of an Irish brogue evident in her speech.

"Thank you." He continued to talk to her, never once glancing down at his paper, even though he had placed it neatly in front of him. "Mrs. O'Hara, are you aware of the nature of this case?"

"Oh yes, sir, a shame it is," Mrs. O'Hara answered solemnly, her face screwing up into an expression somewhere between disgust and sadness.

"It seems, ma'am, that you are well aware of the case. Do you think you could render a fair judgment in this case?"

"Yes, sir. I do," the woman stated without hesitation. Faith glanced in Jim's direction long enough to see him raise his eyebrow slightly over the rim of his spectacles.

"Mrs. O'Hara, could you tell us what your occupation is?" Jim asked as though he was inquiring about the weather. The old woman's eyes lit up as she gladly answered.

"I am the housekeeper for Father Johnson at St. Theresa's Church." The pride in her voice was evident, and Faith leaned over the table to look closely at her. She would be fabulous on a jury of this sort. But Faith's guard was up: Mrs. O'Hara was too good to be true and Jim knew it.

"How long have you been working for Father Johnson?" Jim asked, an edge coming into his voice.

"Sixteen years next week, sir," Mrs. O'Hara answered, unaware of Jim's change in attitude toward her.

"Then can we assume you are a Catholic, Mrs. O'Hara, and as such governed by a strict moral code that...."

"Objection, Your Honor." Faith was out of her seat, hand raised as though she could physically wipe away the offending question. "Your Honor, there's no need to get into Mrs. O'Hara's personal, religious feelings at this time."

"Your Honor," Jim shot back, his eyes forward-looking at the judge, ignoring Faith's tense stance at the table to his left. "May we approach the side bar?" Judge Hardison flicked his wrist indicating they could approach, turning the microphone in front of him to the side as Jim and Faith made their way to the side of the bench.

Faith noted Mrs. O'Hara's surprised and hurt expression as she passed but took no time to flash a consoling smile in her direction. All of her energies were focused on the man moving ahead of her. His gait was purposeful, his shoulders tensed and squared under the deep suit of blue. But Faith did not allow her conscious mind to dwell on him as she took her place beside him as they stood beneath the judge's bench.

"Your Honor," Jim began as soon as they stood stationary, "I must challenge for case in the cause of Mrs. O'Hara."

"Your Honor"—Faith immediately grabbed the man's attention—"Mrs. O'Hara has already indicated that she believes she can provide fair judgment in this case...."

"Your Honor"—Jim's verbal Ping-Pong was excellent, and Faith's mind raced, knowing she would have to cut off whatever objection was made—"you yourself saw how she reacted when asked about her knowledge of the nature of this case, and her occupation would make it very difficult for her not to make moral, rather than legal, judgments regarding my client. How could she possibly return to a rectory each night, work with a priest and not make that kind of judgment?"

"Your Honor." Once again Faith made a stand. "Mrs. O'Hara has given no indication that she is prejudiced in any manner. Counsel has had his chance to examine this lady, and she has been cooperative and straightforward."

"Judge Hardison," Jim countered, "I believe in this instance we must look beyond her simple answers."

"Your Honor," Faith said, exaggerated exasperation dripping from her voice, "this is ridiculous. If we're going to examine facial expressions and religious convictions, then...."

"Miss Karell," the judge spoke, cutting off any further discussion. Glancing back at Mrs. O'Hara who strained to hear what they were saying, he lowered his voice a bit as he continued, "I believe in this instance Mr. Stanten has made a very interesting point. His motion to excuse the juror is granted."

"But Your Honor," Faith objected vehemently.

"Miss Karell, I believe you heard my ruling." Hardison looked at Faith sharply, then turned back and adjusted the microphone, dismissing them both with a "Return to your seats."

Faith opened her mouth once more, then closed it, knowing that further objections were useless. Jim had already left the side bar when she turned and made her way back to her seat, aware that his eyes followed her as she went. But her anger at the loss of this juror protected her from feeling the intensity of his gaze.

"Mrs. O'Hara," the judge was saying as Faith took her seat, "thank you very much, but your services will not be needed."

"I'm sorry, sir," the woman said as she left her chair.

"We are, too, Mrs. O'Hara." Judge Hardison smiled down on her as she passed. It warmed his heart when one of these good people was saddened by the fact that they would not be serving on a jury. So many of them tried to disregard their duty. Then, turning back to the courtroom as Mrs. O'Hara disappeared behind the door from which she had come, he addressed the courtroom again.

"Counsel, it is now eleven thirty-five. I suggest we break for lunch. We are three quarters of the way there. When we resume, I would appreciate it if you would keep your questions brief during the afternoon session so that we can find five more acceptable jurors and alternates before the sun sets and get on with this trial, saving a bit of the taxpayers' money."

"Yes, Your Honor," they replied in unison, each bowing slightly as the judge left for chambers. No one who ever appeared in a federal courtroom was sure why they did such a thing. It was simply a reaction to the pomp the black-robed judge seemed to command.

Gathering up their papers, Jim and Faith turned toward the door at the same time. As he stood back to let her pass before him, he whispered to her, "You look lovely this morning. Did you miss me?" Shooting a glance over her shoulder, Faith tried to give him a stern look but instead only communicated her exasperation and her adoration. Faith couldn't help letting the remembrance of Jim's strong naked body play across her mind as they walked down the aisle to the door.

They had reached the outer corridor and Faith turned to wait for Mark. "I'll have to talk to you later, Jim," she said reluctantly as Mark approached and took her arm.

"Stanten, nice to see you again." Mark fairly sneered the greeting.

"MacMillan" was Jim's only answer as he nodded and turned on his heel with a last look at Faith.

"Why don't we just grab a bite at the Federal Employees' Cafeteria?" Faith said absentmindedly to Mark as she slowly followed Jim down the hall, her eyes on him every moment.

"All right by me," he answered. Mark didn't look at her as he spoke but continued to watch the handsomely dressed figure of Jim Stanten as it disappeared down the hall. Taking her arm as they walked in silence, Mark finally led her into the loud cafeteria. They wound their way through the lines, checking out and finally settling themselves in as quiet a corner as they could find.

Faith immediately attacked her salad. The cheese and turkey on top were stale and the lettuce wilted. What else could she expect from a government cafeteria? In a show of unusual temperment she threw down her fork and rested her chin on the palm of her upturned hand. Mark watched her surreptitiously as he nibbled at his sandwich. Finally replacing it on his plate, he crossed his arms on the table in front of him.

"All right, let's get it out in the open. I'm a jerk. I apologize. I didn't mean to come on so strong the other night and I apologize. Really, Faith, I do. I don't know what came over me. I can usually hold my liquor better than that," he finished somberly.

Faith stared at the man across from her, trying to discern the depth of his sincerity. She didn't blink, no expression crossed her face and Mark squirmed uncomfortably in his chair.

"Faith, I said I was sorry. Stop looking like some zombie out for revenge. I mean what I say. You know I would never hurt you. Can't you forgive me?" Mark's voice was tense and Faith suddenly realized that she had not even been thinking about the other night. She was considering Mark's character in total.

"I'm sorry. I forgive you. I'm just sorry it had to

happen at all. We've worked together for so long, had fun when we went out. It was really awful to see the other side of you," Faith said without rancor, only sorrow that they should have come to this. Then with a sigh of frustration, she continued, "Oh, Mark, it's just that that little scene only added to everything else on my mind. Everything's been bothering me lately."

"Hey, you can't feel like that," Mark said with sudden vehemence, straightening in his chair. "The way Stanten's been oozing his charm around the courtroom, you can't afford to let 'everything' bother you." Faith looked at him defiantly. How dare he lecture her when part of the everything that was bothering her was him! How dare he try to tell her her job!

"Look, you just take care of your end and I'll take care of mine. I've got eyes and ears, too, you know. I can see what's happening and I'll take care of it." She snapped the words at him but, strangely, felt no remorse.

"Okay. Don't worry about me. All I want is to put Bennett away for a good long time. Now eat your salad; we've got to get back in there in fifteen minutes." Once again he picked up his sandwich and Faith watched him, fighting with herself, wondering if she should question him about the perjury charge.

"Mark," she started hesitantly again, "how far would you go to put Bennett in jail?" A little casual digging couldn't hurt, and it might help clear up at least one question in her mind.

"As far as need be."

"What does that mean, 'as far as need be'?" She continued pushing him for an answer.

"Just what I said. I'll do whatever I have to to get that scum and everyone like him off the street. Isn't that what you want, too? Aren't you pulling out all the stops? We both want the same thing—to see that guy get what's coming to him." His voice was frantic with self-righteousness and anger, and Faith was afraid of what his reaction meant, afraid that the others in the cafeteria might hear.

"You're right," Faith said soothingly as though she were trying to calm an angry child. "I just wanted to make sure your tactics were always within the law. You would never consider anything that wasn't above-board, would you? If you would, tell me now before we get into this any deeper." Mark looked at her suspiciously, the color draining from his face.

"What are you trying to say, Faith?" His voice was hushed now, but there was an edge of caution to it. Faith began to wonder if maybe, just maybe, Jim had been right. Mark was acting strangely. Suddenly Mark's face brightened and he rushed on, his voice gratingly cheery before she could answer his question. Was he trying to throw her off the track, away from her line of questioning?

"Besides," he said, "what difference would it make as long as the guy was convicted? You know I'd never do anything but stretch the power a little bit. So," he sighed, putting his napkin on the table and pushing away his half-finished sandwich, "what else is there to say?"

Then, as though he had just been totally shocked at the time indicated on his watch, he patted her hand quickly, "Hey, look at that! It's already time to go."

Mark rose and started toward the door of the cafeteria, leaving Faith to follow slowly, more confused than ever by the conversation and his change of mood. Could it be that she couldn't count on Mark anymore? Had he carried his quest for justice too far in certain instances, just as he had carried his feelings for her too far? She almost didn't want to know, but she would have to press for an answer, she understood that now, but it would have to be later. How naive was she? she wondered as they completed the short walk to the courtroom and resumed their seats. The other side used every talent at their disposal to free their clients, so why shouldn't her side do the same? But was that right? Could justice ever be served in that manner?

The law certainly wasn't blameless with its many loopholes. It almost asked for lawyers and agents and defendants to use it as though, in the search to cover all the bases, it had simply extended the field. No amount of rationalization, however, could ease the doubt and pain in her mind regarding Mark. She lived to the letter of the law, didn't try to turn it around to suit her needs, and she always thought he did the same. She could almost physically feel her confidence in him crumbling as the prospective jurors resumed their seats.

Pushing those thoughts out of her mind, she sat straighter in her chair, smoothing her skirt as she did so. Instinctively her head turned toward the door of the courtroom as she heard it open. Jim was back. They would start again. But before he entered the room, Faith saw him reach for something, a woman, his hand on her shoulder. She was as beautiful as the blonde who had accompanied him to the party at Jenkins, VonDerlieth and Jenkins, only this one was a striking redhead. Faith had seen her before; she was Judge Haig's secretary. Quickly the woman leaned over and kissed Jim lightly on the cheek. In a millisecond it was over, and Jim was walking down the center aisle of the room toward the defense table, smiling at her as though he were walking toward the altar.

Embarrassed that she had witnessed the scene between him and the woman, Faith smiled back weakly and turned toward the front of the room. She could not pinpoint her feelings. Jealousy? Sadness? Disappointment? But why would she be feeling any of those things? After all, they had made no real commitment to each other, and Jim certainly must have a number of women who would be wondering what happened to him if he suddenly dropped out of sight. Nonetheless, the dull throb in her heart, the swelling hurt, could not be put off, and she prayed that the rest of the day would prove to be so hectic that she would not have to worry about Jim or Mark or herself.

There had been no need for the plea, however; the rest of the afternoon proved to be even more of a rush than she had ever anticipated. The last three jurors were a problem. Defense and prosecution could not agree until finally, as the hands of the clock moved toward five, they were able to accept three in a row.

As she and Mark packed up their papers and books, Faith reviewed the jury. Not bad in the final analysis: There were only three people who were not married and didn't have children; nine that could and would, she hoped, empathize with little Meg Cortland because of the ages of their own children. The trial certainly wouldn't turn on their feelings, but it might be swayed because of it. Her spirits were a bit revived by the time she walked through the door into the quiet hallway. Mark was right behind her and Jim had left without a word a few minutes before.

"You want to get a drink before you head home?" Mark ventured as they walked slowly down the hall, the only sound that of their heels clicking on the marble floors.

"No, thanks; I'm kind of tired and I've got to stop back at the office," she said as they turned the corner and entered the short hall that housed the numerous elevators. As they both looked up at the floor dial, they were startled by a cheerful, though quiet, voice that hailed them.

"Faith, MacMillan, can you hold it?" It was Jim Stanten who seemed to appear from nowhere and now stood close to Faith.

"Which one? She's going up, I'm going down," Mark answered rather surlily. Faith threw him a reprimanding look. Goodness, but he was changing before her eyes. Where was the fairly quiet, dedicated agent she had worked with for so long?

"Why up, of course," Jim said as at that moment the doors of the elevator slid open and Faith stepped in followed closely by Jim.

"See you tomorrow, Mark," Faith said solemnly as the door closed once again on Mark's hostile face.

Suddenly, just as the elevator began to rise, it came

to a jolting halt. Jim had pressed the stop button and was smiling at her, lounging casually against the control panel.

"Now I've got you all to myself, even if it is for just a few minutes," he said rakishly.

"What are you doing? Start that right now," her tired voice demanded. Her request had an immediate effect on Jim, and he moved across the small cage, taking her in his arms.

"I'm so sorry. I know it's been a rough day," he said, running his hands over her carefully knotted hair as she sagged into him for an instant.

"It's your job; I'm not blaming you," she answered, the exhaustion now overtaking her. "I just want to go pick up a few things at the office and go home, okay?"

"All right," Jim said moving away from her and retrieving his briefcase. "I just thought you might like to have some dinner or a drink. I just thought you may want to be with me."

Faith was surprised that he seemed so totally dejected by her rejection, but she was too tired to think about it now. She couldn't think of anything more wonderful than snuggling in his arms, making love and falling asleep only to wake and find him there in the morning... if they weren't adversaries now. If she were to be truthful to herself, she would have identified the fear she was feeling.

Until then she had won her cases easily, been lulled into complacency by her own press, believing that she could not fail because right was on her side. Now she wasn't sure. The man who defended the evil ones was also the man she loved, and Faith was beginning to find it increasingly difficult to tell one man from the other. He was a chameleon: so damned believable as he slipped from one persona to another, one woman to another. Stop it, she commanded herself. That was unfair. He had only taken the redhead to lunch, not had a steaming love affair in forty-five minutes. She smiled at him, her mouth tinged with sadness as she looked into his eyes.

"I really do appreciate the offer. I can't think of anything nicer than being with you." His face brightened and he hugged her closer, but she pulled away and moved to the elevator panel where she pushed the button and the cage started its climb.

"I just think it might be better if we don't see each other on a personal level for a while, at least until this trial is over." Her heart was breaking and she could not bear to look at him. Why did she always have to say and do the right thing, she wondered to herself as the last words escaped her lips and the doors opened.

"But, Faith"—Jim's hand covered hers as he held the door back—"that's at least another two weeks!" His surprise and disappointment were evident and Faith was touched.

"I know, but I really think it's best. I just don't need the added involvement right now." She was pleading with him and he began reluctantly to back off.

"I do understand, dear Faith. I promise I won't make another move toward you until this whole thing is over." She could feel the pressure of his hand on hers as his body began to move. In an instant his lips had covered hers gently, and she felt herself succumbing to him once again. His kiss spoke louder than any words, and Faith knew that eventually it would be all right, eventually there would be time for them as people, not attorneys. Had he not backed away only a moment later, she would have gone with him, forgotten the trial and only indulged herself in the comfort of his arms.

"Thanks," she said softly, trying to hide the blush that was rising to her cheeks, turning her head and glancing down the hall. Jim misread her look into the dark and quietly addressed her.

"Do you want me to come with you? It can get pretty spooky here when everyone has gone home." His tone was one of concern, and she had no doubt that his offer was made with the best of intentions.

"No," she said quickly, "no thanks. I do appreciate the offer, though." Then it was her turn. Unable to leave him without touching his flesh one more time, the last time for many days, she leaned into the elevator and kissed him lightly. Then backing out of the elevator, she allowed the door to close as her eyes held his for one more lingering moment.

He seemed to care so much. Faith could not believe his attention to her was an act, one that would end when the final judgment was passed down on Robert Bennett.

She refused to believe it. Thoughts of Jim Stanten were immediately pushed out of her mind, though, as she entered her office. All was quiet and dark except for her office: From under the door she saw a soft, steady light.

Faith's heart beat faster. Should she go for a marshal? After all, it wasn't unusual for a defendant like Bennett to pull out all the stops in order to put an end to a case like this one. Could he really have sent one of his goons to her office? She hesitated, trying to decide what to do.

Shaking her head as she walked with a determined step toward her office, she decided she had nothing to fear, at least not at this point. Jim had been brilliant and they were only at the jury selection process anyway. If Bennett had any ideas about harming her, it would come much later and only if he thought there was no other way. Everyone knew that harming a prosecutor was usually out of the question. If the defense lost, it was the poor defender who garnered the wrath of a man like Bennett.

The thought made Faith's blood run cold. If she won, Jim might somehow be in danger. If she lost, Bennett would go free. Why did she have to care so much about each of the two most important things in her life—Jim and winning the case.

Slowly she reached out toward the door of her office and turned the knob. Faith hadn't realized that she was holding her breath until it all came out in one relieved sigh. In her miserable old chair Darcy sat, feet propped up on the desk, reading a paperback novel.

"You scared the living daylights out of me, Darcy Barber!" Faith hollered at the woman. "What are you still doing here?"

"No need to get all upset," the woman answered laconically. "I just thought you might like to have someone to talk to after a long day. I know your mom and dad are out of town. Who else are you going to talk to?'' Darcy's black eyes looked Faith up and down, and she got up heavily from the chair.

"Honey, you look even worse that I thought you would,'' the older woman said, her voice concerned. "Come sit here and I'll get you some tea.'' Before she let Faith decline her offer, Darcy was gone. Moving around the back of her desk, Faith sat down in the warm chair and wondered how long her secretary had been using her office. Not that she minded. It was sort of comforting to come back to a warm chair. Unbidden, the thought that it would be nice to go home to a warm bed and Jim flitted through her mind.

Darcy came back into the room, still talking about something or other, and set a mug of steaming tea in front of Faith. She backed off and sat down in the green chair opposite the desk, searching Faith's face.

"Faith,'' she said offhandedly, her tone cheery but serious, as Faith looked up, "you've got to stop taking this all so seriously, you know. You're going to get sick if you don't watch it.''

"I know. But there doesn't seem to be a whole lot I can do about it. I guess I was born responsible.'' The remorse in her voice was evident and Darcy wondered what the lady was mourning for.

"How's Mr. Stanten?'' the black woman queried.

"Tough, but I didn't expect anything less.''

"That's not what I meant, you little idiot.'' The spirit was back in her voice and Faith smiled at her friend.

"He's tough in that area, too. I can't seem to get

him out of my mind," Faith admitted a bit reluctantly.

"Don't try, honey," Darcy retorted excitedly. "He's some looker even though he does lie down with dogs." Darcy cackled at her turn of phrase, and Faith found herself taking exception to her statement.

"It's not like that, Darcy; he feels that everyone has a right to a defense. He really believes it." Faith was excited by the challenging words of her secretary, and Darcy only broadened her grin.

"I knew it, I knew it. You're in love with that sucker," she said, waggling her finger at Faith's defensive attitude.

"Don't be absurd," she said, trying to hide the truth. "Certainly I find him attractive. What woman wouldn't? But that doesn't constitute love. Besides, he's got a lot of women." The thought of the lunchtime redhead crashed through her mind like a bullet, only to be followed by the gentler idea of his kiss in the elevator.

"Well, you're better than any of them and don't you forget it," Darcy retorted, her nose in the air.

"I don't know about that, but there are other things to consider. We're worlds apart, you know... the way we live, the way we approach life...." Faith faltered, unable to find the words that would express her concern over her growing feeling toward Jim Stanten. When she did try to explain, all her objections seemed so weak, so ridiculous, next to the possibility of finding love.

"Let me tell you something, Miss Karell." Faith smiled. It was so funny to listen to Darcy at times.

Every now and then, when she was getting ready to lecture Faith, she would use the formal Miss.

"My man and I are so different... different as night and day," she went on hurriedly. "He's so quiet. Why, I had to practically drag him to the altar because he thought it could never work out—loudmouth of the year and fine, refined gentleman like him. But drag him I did because I knew it would work... deep in here." She pointed to her ample chest, obviously indicating her heart. "I knew that I couldn't live without that man. He gave me such a greater view of life. I never dreamed life could be so wonderful. Now four kids later, you think he's sorry? Hell, no. I taught him how to laugh, how to make jokes, and I loved him better than anyone could. Now when you start thinking crazy like you and Mr. Stanten have too many differences, you just remember old Darcy, okay?" She leaned back in her chair, exhausted by her sermon, but still smiling.

"Why, you old fox," Faith said laughingly. "I thought you didn't like Jim Stanten."

"That's before I knew you liked him in a personal way. When he was just a picture in the papers or on the other side of the courtroom, I could say anything I wanted."

"Okay, I'll think about what you said, but now, if you don't mind, I'd like to go home and you should get, too," Faith said, rising from her chair.

By the time the women parted, the street in front of the courthouse was almost deserted. The large black woman turned toward the bus stop and headed home to a husband who loved her. The petite lady in the businesslike suit crossed the street and found her car in the parking lot. Starting the engine, she, too, headed home but to a house that was dark and lonely.

## Chapter Seven

There are some days in Southern California that are strictly made in heaven. Even the normal bright and warming weather cannot hold a candle to those rare mornings when a sweetness settles over the entire land from the dirty streets of downtown to the sleepy bedroom communities of the valley. Today, Faith observed as she sat with her morning coffee, gazing out the small window that faced the beach, was just such a day. Somewhere birds were singing, announcing the lifting of the smog as though, without the heavy blanket of gray matter, they could finally enjoy their song. Even Bailiff seemed to have a gentleness unusual to him as he settled at her feet, unmoving, perfectly content to enjoy the company of his mistress. This was the kind of day that made Faith wish she was one of those valley women who sent their men off to work and took the kids to the park.

Finally dismissing her daydreams, she turned her attention back to the morning paper and sighed a contented sigh. For months Faith had been under the spell of the Bennett trial, but today she could finally sense the normalcy return to her. Possibly it was the weather, but more than likely it was the simple fact that for two days she had been able to put the trial out of her mind.

Judge Hardison had granted Jim Stanten a continuance after the jury selection. A minor matter. Other than the fact that she would have to wait a few days longer to expose Bennett for what he was, there was nothing to worry about. Initially though, Faith had felt as if she was drowning. Her momentum had built to a feverish pitch, and she had been ready to fight, ready to pull out all the stops in the courtroom.

Then, when the continuance had been granted, she had felt as though the rug had been pulled out from under her. Immediately she set to work reviewing, rewriting, reediting all the material she had collected for the trial. It wasn't until Tuesday night that Faith realized she could relax: She had done her homework, she knew the case backward and forward. All was well. The only thing she had to do now was wait for the final confrontation.

Now it was Thursday and she didn't have to be at the office until the following day. Today was for her and Meg Cortland—the meeting Faith had been waiting for. Today she would have to decide whether or not she could put the little girl on the stand. She was ready for the day ahead. She felt relaxed, released from the tension that had been building everyday since she first opened the file on Bennett, since she was first aware of Jim Stanten.

Even Jim, dear Jim, seemed far away from her as she sat in the bright yellow kitchen. Perusing the paper, she lingered over the section that had a particularly interesting letter for Dear Abby and realized that the memory of Jim had simply settled in her heart and mind. Nodding her head in silent agreement with Abby's answer, she turned the pages and laconically perused the headlines and the ads. Buffums was having a sale on sheets, and she filed away a mental note to pick up a set or two if the trial ended before the sale. For now, though, she could not afford to expend valuable energy trying to set her house in order when it was the courtroom she must attend to.

Faith's peace with herself was almost complete this day. She knew that it was Meg Cortland who was going to bend, open up, and not she who was destined to lose this bittersweet battle that was about to be fought. Faith only wished there was another way as she folded the paper and reached down to casually caress the cat. But there was none. Meg Cortland would have to testify. She would have to sit in that big witness box, scared and unsure, and Faith would have to make her believe that everything was all right, make her believe in herself. It was a hard task but not impossible, Faith decided.

Had she allowed herself to consider the ramifications of her actions, Faith would have admitted her own fear. She was playing with a life already torn by lies and disappointment. If she could not convince Meg Cortland of her sincere wish to help her, she might just lose the most important trial of her career.

"Well, Bailiff," Faith said, addressing the cat once more as her confidant, "I hope I handle this right. I don't think I could live with myself if this backfires."

Bailiff raised his head and tilted it to the side. Faith almost thought she saw a look of concern on the exotic white face, but in an instant the cat had once again lowered its head and closed its eyes. It was time for her to go.

Faith rinsed out her juice glass and coffee cup, slowly dried her hands on the tea towel hanging on the refrigerator door and left the sunny kitchen.

Ten minutes later the doors were locked and Faith was whizzing down the almost-empty mid-week freeway, glad that she was free for the day, yet somehow dreading the meeting that was to come. Unconsciously she held onto the bag that lay on the seat beside her. Inside was the beautiful dress she had bought for a beautiful, sad young girl.

She made the drive to Long Beach in record time, and Mrs. Jackson saw them off as Faith settled Meg, still silent and foreboding, in the little car. Waving to the woman on the porch, Faith started the car, realizing, with panic rising in her breast, that she and Meg were finally alone together.

Now, as they sat on the sand of the Belmont Shore Bay, Faith's concern still had not subsided. After more than an hour, Meg still did not speak a word. Faith was running out of things to say to her. She felt as though she were the only player in a very long one-act play. Finally, her courage waning in the face of her challenging little friend, Faith decided to play her trump card—the dress.

"Meg," she began hesitantly, "I have to leave for just a minute. Will you be all right here by yourself?"

The inquiry seemed to fall on deaf ears, and receiving no reply, Faith stood up slowly and shielded her eyes against the glorious sun. Up and down the beach she could see only a few people scattered on big bright towels. Weekdays were the best time to come to the beach, hardly anyone was ever there. No loud radios, no teenagers making out shamelessly, no muscle men showing off for the groupies that inevitably gathered by the seashore. Lowering her hand, she looked down once more at the little blond-headed girl. "Meg, is it all right if I go away for a minute or so?" Faith ventured once again. "I won't be long." As she watched, the little head nodded almost imperceptibly.

Shrugging her shoulders in defeat, Faith walked away wishing for all the world that Meg would have simply looked at her or spoken one word so that she would feel better about leaving her behind, even for a little while. Well, maybe they both needed to be alone with their thoughts. After all, ten-year-olds had a lot to think about when they were normal kids and even more when they had been through what Meg had. And she wasn't a toddler. If anyone could take care of herself, it was Meg.

It took longer to walk to the car than Faith had remembered, and once she located the Volkswagen crunched in between two vans, both sporting the garish window paintings that had become so popular with teenagers, she quickly retrieved the package and began the trek back to the beach.

She was gone longer than she had anticipated. Cursing herself, she rushed back along the streets, her bearings finally in order as she skirted the quiet avenues. Stopping for just a moment, she ordered two deep-fried burritos . . . she was hungry and maybe Meg was, too. Carrying her package under one arm and the burritos, hot and steaming, in her cupped hands, Faith scurried over the burning sand, suddenly feeling refreshed and ready to begin again with the little girl she had left sitting quietly, forlornly, on the white sand.

Faith stopped when she was no more than fifty yards from the pavement. Something was different, but she couldn't put her finger on what it was. The lifeguard still sat at his station looking bored; the young mother with her two children still sat reading her magazine. But something . . . someone . . . was missing.

Meg! It was Meg. She was no longer sitting by the shore. She wasn't sitting where Faith had left her. Trying to quicken her step, she trudged sluggishly over the confining sand, looking everywhere for some sign of Meg. Her breath was coming short now, but she kept up her pace, finally arriving at the exact spot at which they had sat not more than ten minutes earlier. The indentation of their bodies was still evident in the sand, as was the primitive castle Faith had absentmindedly been building as she spoke to Meg. Beside that, Faith's sandals peeked out of the beach half-covered by the warm sand.

"Meg?" Faith called loudly, her voice still under control, her concern not yet evident. "Meg, where are you? I brought you some lunch." Her call fell on deaf ears. Nowhere did anyone turn her head to look at the woman with the burritos and the bag from Bullocks. No one offered a word as to where the little girl had gone.

Panic was beginning to overtake her as the silence extended over the beach. Faith stopped, dropping the food into the silly sandcastle, as the realization of what she was thinking dawned on her.

She was responsible for Meg this day. But her fear encompassed more than the responsibility for a child. It was the thought that only the case mattered, had made her feel protective, and Meg was the cornerstone of that case. Or was there a deeper concern hovering somewhere near her heart? Whatever it was, Faith only knew she had to find the girl fast.

Suddenly her feet had wings. Faith ran up and down the beach, faltering as she tossed her head about trying to scan the sand as she went, looking for any sign of Meg. Her pants were wet from the gentle waves that lapped at her feet as she ran toward the ocean, toward the pounding waves and away from the calm waters of the bay. Now and again she would stop and ask sunbathers if they had seen a girl answering Meg's description. But every time the answer was the same. Sometimes it was polite, other times surly, but always it was no.

Faith flogged herself mentally over and over again. Hadn't Mrs. Jackson warned her that Meg was unpredictable? She should have known a girl who hadn't spoken in weeks wouldn't react normally to being left alone in a strange place. Boy, she was stupid! Faith was beginning to realize that she had let the trial rule her life to the extent she wasn't using her common sense. Up until that moment all she had thought about was herself and beating Jim Stanten.

As she ran, all thoughts of her previous behavior

fled from her mind, only to be replaced by fierce, raw fear for the safety of Meg Cortland. Faith had finally reached the ocean and, seeing no sign of Meg, turned and walked slowly back to the spot where they had parted so long ago. Faith held her head high, squinting her eyes into the shining sun as she continued her search, this time controlling herself, trying to think rationally, trying to put herself in Meg's small shoes. Where would she go? Where would she hide? If she found Meg safe, she promised herself that she would do nothing more to pressure the girl. She just wanted to find her safe.

Then she saw her in the distance. Unbelievably she sat exactly where she had been left. Faith stopped, the water playfully rushing up, dancing at her feet but withdrawing again unnoticed by the small, dark-haired woman. Rubbing her eyes, Faith once again looked into the sun. Had she been imagining it? Was she willing herself to see Meg? No, the girl was there, head bent exactly as it had been when Faith had left her. Before she could even think, Faith broke into a run.

Her feet seemed winged as she fairly skimmed over the cumbersome, uneven sand. In seconds she was beside Meg, the crumpled bag still clutched tightly at her side, her breath coming in hard, rasping gasps. For a moment she simply stood looking down at the mute, unmoving figure; then, as she watched, Meg's head turned upward, the shining hair falling back from her face as she looked directly at Faith, her eyes expressionless.

"Where have you been?" Faith screamed with the

vigor that comes from controlled fear suddenly loosed. "I've been looking all over for you! I thought you had drowned! How could you?" Her entire body shook as she confronted the little girl who seemed to wince under very harshly spoken words.

The implications of the almost unnoticeable action pierced Faith's mind. *What am I doing?* she thought to herself. *I must be scaring her out of her wits!*

Raising her face to the unblemished sky, Faith breathed deeply, trying to regain her composure before once again addressing Meg. Then she heard the girl's voice, no more than a feathery whisper carried through the still air. Faith's head snapped back, all her attention now focused on the child who sat at her feet.

Bending her knees, she dropped the package in the sand and took Meg gently by the shoulders.

"What is it?" she said quietly. "What is it, Meg? Where have you been?"

The little girl shrank back and Faith wondered if Meg thought she was going to be forced to speak. Instead she repeated again what she had said, her scrawny shoulders tensing and straightening, almost defiant.

"I had to go to the bathroom" were her only words. Softly spoken though they were, Faith noted the courage with which they were said and her heart opened to Meg. Here truly was a girl with courage, a self-sufficient little bundle. Much more than certainly Faith herself possessed. She couldn't even get her own life straight, and all she had to worry about was a job and how to handle the affection of a handsome and generous man. Here was a child who had weathered the wars of the human spirit and the physical body. What lessons one could learn if only Meg would open up.

Faith released the slender shoulders only long enough to gather Meg Cortland into her arms and whisper into the mass of hair, "Did you find the bathroom, darling?"

Perhaps to an outsider the question spoken so fervently would have sounded ridiculous, even ludicrous, but to Faith it was only the beginning of the very long process of getting to know Meg Cortland. The shorter process of loving her had already begun.

"Listen, sweetheart," Faith said, licking some of the refried beans from her fingers, "what do you say to going over to the park for a few minutes? We could ride on the swings and they even have a merry-go-round."

Meg seemed to consider the proposition for a moment and then nodded her head enthusiastically. Faith was pleased by the response and hopeful that the rest of the day would prove to be fruitful. After all, it was only noon and they wouldn't have to head home for another four hours. They ate in silence for a few minutes more before Faith felt a tug on her sleeve.

"Yes?" She tried not to sound too hopeful as she looked down at the girl. She didn't want to scare Meg away just as she was beginning to show some life.

"What's in the bag?" Meg asked shyly, almost fearfully as she now eyed the torn parcel.

Faith looked down and noticed that the fabric of the pretty dress was peeking through a hole in the side of the bag. Amused that curiosity finally got the best of Meg, Faith played up the drama for a little while longer, hoping to draw out the conversation.

"Oh," she said nonchalantly, "nothing much. Just something I thought you might like. But it's probably not."

Meg sat silently for a moment, the big burrito oozing cheese and beans onto her lap, but she didn't even seem to notice as she looked from the bag to Faith.

"How do you know I wouldn't like it?" Faith's heart leaped for joy. It was more than she could have expected. Meg was actually asking her questions, egging her on instead of the other way around.

"Well, you don't seem to be interested in much of anything," Faith went on as though they had been friends for years. "I mean you didn't even tell me when you were going to leave the beach. I guess you're not much interested in how I feel about things, so you probably wouldn't want to know what I brought you. After all, if you don't like me, you won't like my present, right?" Faith held her breath. She knew she was gambling, but it would be worth it if her ploy worked. The funny thing was Faith wasn't even thinking about how much she needed the little girl for the trial. She was simply thinking how much she needed Meg's trust... period.

Once again Meg resumed her attack on the burrito, this time slowly, thoughtfully. Faith, too, pretended to be interested in her food and took a long, cool drink of her Coke, all the while watching Meg out of the corner of her eye.

Then, putting down her snack with great ceremony, Meg laid her hands in her lap and lowered her head, once again contemplating the ground. Faith waited, wondering what the outcome would be. Had she gone too far, pushed too hard? Was Meg now hurt by the game and withdrawing into herself once again? Then the girl lifted her face and straightened her shoulders.

"I like you," she said in a clearly sincere and serious voice, "and I bet I'd like whatever you brought me. Even if I didn't, I wouldn't tell you because I really like you."

Faith's face broke into a wide grin. Her face fairly sparkled with delight as she looked down at Meg Cortland. No longer was her countenance marred by the seemingly permanent shadow that Faith had seen there before. Instead there was only pleasure, innocent childish pleasure as the girl and the woman smiled at one another. Wiping her hands on the small napkin that lay in her lap, Faith reached for the bag.

"Well," she said brightly, "in that case I think you better have this." Without further ado she handed the bag to Meg who held it gently for a minute and then slowly opened the package.

A myriad emotions played over the child's face. Meg's eyes opened wide as she almost reverently pulled the dress out so that she could inspect it closely. Her hands played over the crisp cotton and petted the velvet ribbon at the neck. Faith thought she saw a bit of suspicion float across her eyes, but as soon as she bestowed another smile and a reassuring pat on Meg's arm, the look soon left only to be replaced by sheer excitement.

"I never had anything so beautiful," Meg said, her voice filled with hushed awe. "Is it really mine?"

"Certainly it is," Faith answered, pleased that she had taken the time to pick something extra special for Meg. "I hope you like it."

The girl nodded and clutched the dress to her boyish chest. All thoughts of lunch seemed to have left Meg's head as she simply sat in the sunlight, caressing the gift.

Now the silence between them was a happy one, born not of fear or apprehension, but of trust and friendship. Faith was hard pressed to understand her feelings for the little waif who had just been another player in the current drama that was her life. But something special was growing inside her.

It wasn't until she had left Meg with the Jacksons once again that a thought began to formulate in her mind. The idea was that for once in her life she would do something totally good, something not related to her profession, to good or evil. Faith didn't want to be alone, she knew that. Jim was someone she could think about but she would not be able to control what was to happen to them. If it were meant to be, then it would be. Perhaps lovers, perhaps more, but she could control that situation only so far. Meg was a different matter. She was alone, frightened. She needed someone to love her and Faith needed someone to love.

It wasn't until Faith was halfway home that the idea began to take on a life of its own in her mind. First it was slow, almost nonexistent, a silent creature crawling about in her brain. Then as it grew, becoming clearer and clearer, Faith was at first astonished, then incredulous at its implications. The freeway towns whizzed by, but Faith did not see them, was unaware that she was even driving past them, as she considered more and more the overwhelming idea. She and Meg. Why not Meg... Meg... Meg Karell? Why not?

Faith wanted to holler with delight as the thought of adopting Meg Cortland overtook her completely. Instead, though, she swerved her car onto the shoulder of the freeway, oblivious to the other cars that were speeding past her as she sat in the gathering dusk of the day.

She could think of no one else in the world who needed Meg more than herself. It would be hard, of course. There would be financial worries, sharing the house with someone else, not being able to work too late every night, school. All those drawbacks seemed trivial to Faith as she mulled the situation over and over again in her mind. After all, she had everything that really counted. Faith wanted a child so much, desperately needed to love someone who would love her back for who she was. She had no doubt that she could be the kind of loving, caring mother that a girl like Meg needed. After all, didn't she know everything there was to know about the little girl? What better way to start a relationship than that?

But she was alone, she thought sadly. So why not alone, came the answer. There were plenty of women on their own, caring for families larger than one child every day of the year. They had been doing it since time immemorial. Faith knew she could, too. With her sense of dedication, her lifelong wish for a child of her own, she knew she would be the perfect candidate to adopt Meg.

Of course, it would be nice to share the experience with someone. To be able to give Meg a mother and a father who cared for her, but right now that was impossible. Or was it? She cared for Jim Stanten more deeply than anyone on the earth. And it seemed that her feelings were returned. But could she honestly tell herself that she could live with the man who was trying to help Robert Bennett? The answer did not come easily. All her years of prejudice against attorneys like him came to the forefront, to be fought back in her mind as she admitted her deep attraction for him... even love for him. There was no denying it. Faith could not live without either of them. Jim and Meg were meant to be a part of her life, but only Meg was within reach.

Suddenly a knock on the window disturbed her thinking, and Faith looked over into the eyes of a policeman who was peering through the window at her. She felt the color rise to her cheeks as she slowly rolled down the window and spoke to him.

"Is there anything wrong, officer?" she queried, knowing full well why he had stopped.

"I was just about to ask you the same thing, miss," he said in a pleasant, even voice.

"Oh, you mean sitting here on the shoulder." Faith was flustered and didn't quite know how to explain her strange situation. "Oh, well, I was just...."

"May I see your license please, miss?" He was still friendly, but the tone in his voice indicated that Faith had better comply immediately with the request.

Digging into her purse, she pulled out the credential issued to all Assistant U.S. Attorneys, opened it and located her license. She always carried her important identification in the black case with the gold seal. Turning back to the officer, she handed him the well-worn license, but his eyes were not on it. The leather wallet held his attention.

"Do you mind?" he asked, indicating the credential.

"No, of course not," she answered and handed it to him. "You see, officer," she went on, "I thought I heard some knocking under the hood, so I pulled off, and then I guess I was just so overwhelmed by the sunset that I sat and admired it for a minute." Even to Faith the story sounded feeble, but the officer turned away to look at the red and gold sky.

"I see what you mean, Miss Karell," he said, handing back the license and the credentials, "but it would be a better idea to do your gazing somewhere other than the freeway."

"Of course," Faith said, relieved that he had not questioned her further or given her a ticket for stopping unlawfully. The Los Angeles police really were nice guys, she thought as she turned on the ignition and looked up at the craggy-faced man once more.

"Thank you officer; it won't happen again." Her voice was clear but she could still feel the burning color in her face. The man tipped his hand to his helmet and turned as though he were going to walk away, then he stopped and came back to the car.

"I sure do think you people in the U.S. Attorney's office do one heck of a job, ma'am." With that, he was gone.

- Faith was almost sure she would now die of embarrassment. It had been the credential that caused him
to act so kindly. If Mark MacMillan had witnessed
that exchange, Faith was sure he would never let her
live it down. How could she have been so stupid to
think that it was just a man in a uniform being extraor-
dinarily nice? As she pulled off the shoulder and back
into the flow of traffic, Faith stuffed the credential
deep into her purse, vowing that she would buy a
separate wallet for her license.

It wasn't long before Faith completely forgot about
the traffic incident and once again resumed her con-
templation of Meg and the possibility of adoption, If
only her mother and father were in town. She would
have dearly loved to talk to someone about the idea,
get a second opinion. Then she saw it—the Westwood
Boulevard off ramp. Before she even thought, Faith
exited the freeway and headed toward Sunset and Jim
Stanten's beautiful apartment.

It wasn't until she actually sat, parked in front of
the imposing high-rise, that she wondered if she were
doing the right thing. Hadn't she been the one to set
the ground rules? Hadn't she been the one to decline
any contact until the trial was over? And hadn't Jim
been wonderful about keeping the bargain? Or was
he? she wondered. Maybe he really didn't want to be
with her as much as she thought. Maybe he had just
been toying with her and was happily awaiting the
time when she would be out of his life professionally.
Faith dismissed the thought. He could not have made
love to her so tenderly if he really didn't care about
her... a little bit anyway.

The thought converged on her like the shadow of an ominous rain cloud, nonetheless. Well, she finally decided, there was only one way to find out what his feelings were. She had to see him to understand how he felt, and she would see him now. At least, even if he wasn't thrilled to find her on his doorstep, he might give her some insight into her recent decision to adopt Meg. Faith knew she had to talk to someone and it might as well be Jim. Had she been truly honest with herself Faith would have realized that, the moment she rang Jim's bell, Meg was only part of the reason she wanted to see him. But her honor, her pride, would not allow her to acknowledge how deeply she missed him.

There was only one way to find the answers to her questions and Faith slipped out of her car and ran lightly to the door of the apartment complex. Now, as she stood before the silent door, her heart leapt to her throat. He wasn't home. The disappointment engulfed her and Faith once again rang the bell, hoping against hope that perhaps he had simply not heard her first call. Amazingly she felt tears welling inside her. Why had she been so stupid as to set down those guidelines for their courtship? Turning away from the door, Faith slowly began to make her way back to the car. But, before she was even half way down the walk, the intercom sputtered, the words it carried unintelligible. Faith's face broke into a radiant smile as she dashed back toward the porch of the building.

"Jim, it's me...let me in," she said happily into the little mechanical box.

"Faith?" His tone was incredulous. *Naturally he*

*would be surprised,* she thought. *He didn't think he'd see me for weeks.*

"Yes, it's me...let me in," she repeated. A heavy sigh wafted over the mechanism as she heard a buzz and the door clicked to allow her entry.

Faith stood at the elevator, tapping her hands one against the other as she waited for what seemed to be an inordinately long period of time. She wished she could fly or will herself up to his apartment. Now that she was sure she wanted him, sure she wanted Meg, Faith was beside herself with excitement. All concern regarding Jim was pushed out of her mind in defense of her emotions.

The thought that Jim would not accept her with open arms did not exist for her. He wanted her, for he had said so so many times. The earlier concerns that he had taken the exile she had imposed upon him lightly were nowhere to be found now. For the first time in many months, Faith felt as though she had something to live for, and she was going to charge full steam ahead into life. It was her personal existence now that was at stake, everything else could be worked out. Jim's high rolling way of life, his choice of clients, Meg's emotional problems...Faith felt sure that she would be able to conquer any and all obstacles that stood in the way of her happiness.

Had anyone stopped her for just an instant before she entered the elevator and asked her whether or not Meg wanted her or Jim needed her she probably would have turned back. More than likely her courage would have waned and she would have convinced herself to return home, think things through logically.

But there was no one to stop her. No one to put a gentle warning hand on her shoulder as her heart flew before her and the elevator slowly but surely allowed her body to follow.

The doors finally opened and Faith stepped out into the plushly carpeted hall. Self-consciously she ran her hands through her mussed hair and quickly reached into her purse for her compact. Checking her face in the mirror, she noted the high color of her face. She looked as though she had just run a hundred miles to this place. Her lips were slick and glistening and her eyes shone with excitement, pleasure and love. Satisfied that Jim would not be disappointed in her appearance, Faith took a deep breath in an attempt to calm herself, straightened her shoulders and walked determinedly down the hall. Only the half hidden grin betrayed her anxious heart.

Strange, she thought as she approached his door, he wasn't there to meet her. She had been sure that she would have found him lounging casually in the doorway as he had that wonderful Sunday morning. Well, it had taken him a while to answer the bell; maybe he wasn't prepared for visitors. She chuckled to herself as she thought of the possibility that his apartment and his appearance might not be perfect. No one would ever believe it... his whole image was one of perfection at all times. If anyone believed his press clippings, it would seem that he actually slept in his suit.

Lightly she knocked on the door, four quick raps, two slow ones. Faith smiled. She couldn't believe she was playing such a frivolous game. The last time she had indulged in the knocking game was with her sister on a school holiday in Paris. Today she almost expected to hear the prescribed response from the other side of the door. But, there was nothing, only silence. Straining to hear any sign of movement from within, Faith almost pressed her ear to the door. Then she heard the sound of voices from the other side.

It had never occurred to her that he might have company. A Thursday evening usually meant work for her. But she couldn't expect it to mean the same for him. Suddenly rationality set in. What was she doing? She had no idea how he spent his week nights. Their courtship had been so one-sided until then. Maybe she shouldn't be there. After all, hadn't she been the one to preach caution, and here she was planning her life around him, around Meg and neither one of them even knew it.

Suddenly the door opened and Jim stood before her, swathed in a rich burgundy robe, his hair glistening with water, combed back sleekly from his square face, his wire frame glasses firmly in place.

Faith nearly fell back from the door in her embarrassment and surprise. Her hand rose to her throat as though that small action would somehow ease the moment for both of them. Why didn't he smile at her? Shouldn't he be holding out his arms to her? Be happy to see her? The look on his face was not one of anger, thank goodness, only curiosity. His eyes looked quizzically at her, shining behind the black spectacles. Then, finally, he smiled . . . softly, sweetly, and Faith began to giggle.

"I'm sorry. Did I get you out of the shower?" she said through her laughter and relief.

"As a matter of fact, I finished a few minutes ago. However I never considered my appearance was humorous after I had just showered and shaved," he answered lightly, his smile slowly becoming a grin. Faith felt her heart warm under his gaze. He was glad to see her. Then why was she still standing in the hall?

"Oh, you don't look funny at all! I'm just glad to see you," she said gently, hoping this opening would be enough for him to sweep her into his arms. Instead he simply stood before her, his arm still on the doorknob. Well, if he was that surprised, she thought blithely, she would just have to take the initiative. After all, if she could put aside their differences and make a stand as a woman, she could be a little forward.

"Well, I have got some wonderful news for you, and I'm not going to tell you in the hall so...if you don't mind...." With that, Faith's slim, denim-clad body swept past him and into the beautifully decorated apartment.

"Faith, I've got to warn you..." he started to say as he closed the door behind her.

"Well," she cut in, "you are a perfectionist. Even in the middle of the week your apartment is spotless. How do you do it?" She chattered on and he wondered if she had simply not heard him or was ignoring his statement.

"Faith..." He tried again to break in but she was in no mood to heed him; she was giddy with her new-found feminine courage. The news of Meg and her own resolve not to let her professional stance interfere with a relationship with him were just too good to let him break her concentration.

"Jim, you're not going to believe what I've decided to do. I wanted you to be the first to know because . . . ." She hesitated. How could she explain why she needed to be with him? Then the words were out before she had time to consider the proper phraseology. "Because I love you. I don't care . . . ."

Suddenly she stopped, her words cut off as though someone had just clicked off a tape recorder. But it was not a word or look from Jim that curtailed her excited speech. It was the figure of a leggy, blond woman standing in the doorway of Jim's bedroom, clad only in a man's pale blue shirt.

Faith's mouth fell open, the color draining from her face as she stared at the woman. It was Sandy Druid. Casually the blonde sauntered into the room and stood next to Jim. In a show of frustration, he raised his beautifully manicured hands.

"Faith, it isn't what you think," he said calmly, his words clipped. There was no blush of embarrassment in his face, no flustered speech. He was so cool. Only his eyes showed a hint of concern as he stared at the petite, dark-haired woman who still stood alone in the middle of the room. But it could have been a trick of the light. It could have been concern for the other woman.

"It's okay. I should have called," Faith stammered, putting her palms out toward them in an effort to curtail any explanations he might offer. "I'm sorry. For-

give me." With that she moved hurriedly to the door.
Her hand turned the knob and just before she stepped
into the hall, she heard Sandy speak.

"Well, that was curious..." the woman drawled
before the door closed and Faith was mercifully by
herself, walking quickly toward the elevator. This
time the mechanical door answered her call immediately, and in minutes she was rushing to the car, starting it and heading out of Westwood.

Had she been delayed for only a moment, somehow been made to wait for only a second longer, she
would have heard the door to apartment 10A open
and seen a slightly disheveled Jim Stanten rush into
the hallway after her.

# Chapter Eight

Her tears had been all but spent on the ride back to her home in Venice, their flow finally staved by the time she pulled her car into the garage. Only the sound of her deep, dry sobbing could be heard in the still night as she walked slowly through the immaculate little yard and opened the door to the house.

Heavily she fell onto the lush sofa as Bailiff quietly jumped up to greet her. As though he sensed the deep misery of her soul, the usually independent cat snuggled onto her breast and her arms surrounded him, holding him close, sobbing into the cloud of white fur.

How could she have been so stupid! It seemed as though she could never do anything half way. When would she learn to temper her actions with common sense? She couldn't go on living her personal life this way, one day totally self-sufficient, dedicated to her work, the next day ready to take on a little waif of a girl and propose to a man whose life-style she was uncomfortable with, whose ethics she couldn't condone or understand. Sometimes she could be such a dope, she chided herself.

The squirming cat in her arms seemed to sense that Faith had finally recovered from her bout of self-pity and now his services as consoler were unneeded. He moved from her and jumped to the floor, sauntering into the kitchen to hunt for a more private place to nap.

"You, too, Bailiff?" Faith asked wryly. "You're going to leave me high and dry?"

With a heavy sigh Faith dragged herself to the bathroom and looked in the mirror. With a sarcastic chuckle and a hiccup signaling the last vestiges of her tears, she wondered how she could ever compete with one of Los Angeles's glamour queens. Her mascara had run, leaving black rivulets on her face where the tears had mixed with the gooey dark make-up. Her eye shadow was smudged up into her eyebrows and her hair was mussed.

She turned on the cold water and let it run for a moment into the porcelain sink and then bent down, hands cupped, to scoop up the refreshing liquid, letting it splash over her heated skin. The icy cold washed away a part of the sadness she was feeling, making her skin tingle. Faith reached for another handful of the delightfully clear water and was just raising it to her face when the doorbell rang.

"Damn," she said aloud as she reached for the towel and began to buff her face, trying to remove more of the stubborn make-up. Somewhat blinded by her continuing attack on her wet face, Faith stubbed her toe on the doorjamb as she made her way through the living room to answer the insistent bell. She was so depressed she didn't even wonder who it might be until her hand was on the knob and the door was opening.

Never in her wildest dreams would she have expected to see Jim Stanten standing at her door...especially the way he looked. She almost didn't recognize him. His hair was still partially wet, but it had begun to curl and frizz without the benefit of a blow dry styling. Over his worn jeans he sported an old sweater that was torn at the sleeve and on his feet a pair of old sneakers sans socks. Faith was almost too stunned to think. He was probably there to yell at her for dropping in on him like that. Thoughts flew about her mind as she wondered what she would say. She couldn't blame him for being angry; she had acted like a stupid child. Faith could feel her cheeks coloring with embarrassment as he stood before her; his hands in his pockets. In the back of her mind, though, she thought he looked somewhat sheepish, almost embarrassed himself, but she quickly dismissed the thought. What did he have to be embarrassed about?

"Faith—"

"Jim—"

They began simultaneously, both stopping at the sound of the other's voice, both glancing down at the floor and then up again, their eyes finally locking. Faith's heart was pounding in her breast. Even in his present state he was absolutely disarming. Perhaps he was even more attractive...his unkempt state was almost charmingly young and vulnerable. Faith stepped back from the door, wordlessly inviting him in. Holding her breath, whe wondered if he would accept the invitation.

Slowly Jim entered the house, carefully maneuvering around her so that he did not touch her as he passed. With deliberate movements he walked to the couch and sat down, his knees apart, arms clasped and resting on them.

Closing the door softly, Faith took a deep breath before she turned and walked a few steps toward him. She pulled the now damp towel through her hands and then, gathering her courage, she spoke.

"Jim, I have to apologize. That was a silly thing I did...coming to your apartment that way. I don't know what possessed me to barge in on you like that...." The words fell in a torrent, a savage rain of verbiage as her tears once again began to fall.

In a moment he was beside her, his arms wrapped about her slender body. Faith, unresisting, melted into him, her senses assaulted by the clean smell of his hair and his freshly laundered old clothes. It felt so good to be close to him. He was so kind, calmly holding her when she had wronged him, invaded his life so blatantly. Through her tears she could hear the gentle beat of his heart sounding rhythmically in her ear.

"Faith, my darling," he whispered softly into the great mass of tangled, black hair, "it's I who should be apologizing. I handled the whole thing dreadfully."

Faith could hardly believe her ears, and for some unknown reason she thought not only of his words but also of her mascara-drenched tears falling on the silly old sweater. It was amazing; he was actually apologizing to her. But for what?

"I was just so stunned when you showed up at my

door. And then, when you rushed in talking a mile a minute, you didn't give me a chance to explain. I tried to tell you Sandy was there,'' he went on gently.

"It doesn't matter...I had no right....'' Her words skipped a beat as a wayward sob punctuated her sentence.

"You had every right. We mean a lot to each other,'' he answered, his hands running soothingly through her hair as he tried to comfort her. "Sandy is just a friend of mine. We met because we're neighbors. We've gone out more than a few times, but our relationship has always remained that of good friends. On my part, that is. Sandy's always doing little things to try to get my goat. Like showing up on my doorstep dressed the way she was. All she knows how to deal with is her looks. She doesn't know any other way to attract a man.'' His words flowed over her, slowly, as though he knew that he had to remain calm, collected, explaining the situation rationally so that Faith would understand what he was saying. Her head snapped up and she looked at him through a veil of tears.

"It never even crossed my mind to tell you about her habit of dropping in. Many of the neighbors do that in such a closed building. And I certainly never expected the fine, upstanding Faith Karell to come waltzing into my apartment unannounced. How unseemly!'' he continued playfully, his voice still full of apologetic sadness as his strong hand moved to her face and gently wiped away her tears. "You know circumstantial evidence isn't usually the best grounds for a case. You above all people should know that.''

Faith's cheeks reddened with embarrassment as she thought about the scene that must have ensued after her departure. She should have listened to the little voice that told her not to barge in on Jim.

Suddenly his face grew serious, the smile gone from his voice, only to be replaced by sincerity so deep that it stirred Faith to the bone. "I don't tell every woman that I love her, and I don't wait patiently for anyone. But with you, well, things have been different from the start. Faith, I love you. I want you and I wouldn't do anything to hurt you. Sandy just likes to make people think we're more than friends, that's all. You must believe me." A sweet smile appeared about his lips as he continued to try and wipe her tears away completely.

"Are you sure?" Faith hiccupped once again through her almost silent sobs.

"Of course, I am," he answered, "and there's only one way I know to prove it."

Faith looked up at him, wondering what he had in mind. Her arms rose from her sides and she embraced him tentatively, her mind and body thrilling to the feel of his lean body.

"You don't have to prove anything to me. I believe you about Sandy. It's just that I have a hard time imagining why on earth you would want me when you have someone like her at your beck and call." Faith never would have thought that she could play a silly female game like the one she was involved in. She had never fished for a compliment in her life, yet around Jim she needed so much reassurance.

"Well at times like this I find it hard to believe myself," he said. Faith looked up at him, unable to believe what she had heard. "I usually don't date women who have black lines running down their faces," he went on teasingly, making her forget all about Sandy and her embarrassing visit to his apartment only a few hours earlier. Finally it dawned on her that she must really look a sight. Confidence was beginning to flow back into her, and she immediately picked up on his easy bantering.

"You know, you don't look so great yourself, Mr. Defense Attorney," she answered, her tears all dried, her voice soft and sweet as she looked at him through lashes that still glistened with the remains of her sorrow.

"Faith, does it matter? Now we are the same . . . no cars or clothes or fancy apartments to set us apart, no courtroom to divide us. Can't you see how much we are alike? Both of us are caring, sensitive people. Can't you now forget everything that there could be between us in the courtroom and think about what is between us as a man and a woman?" His voice was pleading and the depth of his caring was so evident that Faith thought her heart would break with love. Standing on her toes, she kissed his soft, inviting lips, pulling away only long enough to whisper one thing.

"That's what I came to tell you this afternoon. . . ." But he would not, could not, allow her to finish her sentence, so great was his desire. His lips captured hers, cutting the words off and making her answer him with her desire.

His arms were engulfing her, hers pulling him ever closer until they were as one body. As they shifted their lips, attacked once again, pulled away to enjoy the softness of each other's mouth, all thoughts of Meg dissipated into the electrically charged atmosphere around them.

Faith devoured him, her lips opening and closing as she choked back small sobs, cries of delight this time, cries of such sublime contentment that this was the only way she knew to express them.

Each touch of his finger, each caress of his hand, each touch of his hard, muscled thigh was a magician's wand that drove away the last vestiges of doubt that Faith Karell harbored about her femininity, her desirability, her power to please him more than any other woman on the earth. The love they shared made them peers on a plane above that of the normal world, and Faith moved on that plane with confidence and happiness.

As their lovemaking became more frantic, Jim swept Faith into his arms and carried her through the small house to the shadow-shrouded bedroom. His mustachioed lip nuzzled her face as she snuggled her head deeper into the crook of his neck and Faith sighed with delight. Gently he laid her down and, taking the towel she still held in her hands, softly wiped away the remains of her disturbed make-up before he once again took her in his arms and slowly but expertly proved his love, bringing her to the pinnacle of ecstacy, sustaining each sensation as though their time of love would never end.

The night grew old and Faith fell asleep in his arms, content and thinking only that she should tell him about Meg. But her exhaustion and happiness were so complete that she could not will herself to speak. Instead she succumbed to the delicious protection of his warm and loving body.

For the first time in many weeks, Faith did not dream at all. But even in her deep and restful sleep she was aware of Jim as he lay beside her, lost in his own night thoughts. She awakened an hour before six and lay watching his handsome, sleep-tousled head and soft shoulders, tanned and rounded. Her entire bedroom seemed bathed in new and refreshing light, and she was careful not to move, not to make a sound lest she destroy the wondrous mood that had settled over the entire house. Even Bailiff seemed inordinately quiet as though he knew instinctively that this morning was of grave importance to the well-being of his mistress.

Every once in a while Jim would stir, shifting his head to the right or left. Once his hand reached out and captured her trim, naked waist, and Faith thought she could see a hint of a smile play about his lips as their flesh made contact. Her entire body tingled as she thought of the night before and knew that if she were to pull the covers back from both of them, the last blush of love would still dance about them like an exquisite halo.

In the end it was her contented sigh and the light touch of her slim fingers to his cheek that woke him. His eyes fluttered open and he gazed at her, still groggy from his rest. Then, wordlessly, he reached for her with both hands and pulled her into him. Faith smiled as she nuzzled him, enjoying the feel of him, wondering at his growing desire so early in the morning. As though she hadn't a care in the world, Faith's hands began gently to explore Jim's warm body. Her fingers followed the sloping path of muscle rippling beneath the amber surface of his skin. Softly his lips covered her face with angel kisses, and she almost gave into her own rising need. But she knew that was impossible so early on a workday. There would be time enough during the weekend. Time enough during their lives.

"Enough, my love," she said sweetly, quietly placing her tapered fingers in front of his lips. "It's almost time to go to work."

He groaned in disappointment and released her, falling back onto the pillows of the bed in mock despair.

"Oh, why can't you have a nice cushy job in private practice? Only savages and government attorneys get to work on time," he said lightheartedly.

Strangely enough Faith felt no anger at his words and only chuckled along with his lament. She knew he was not putting her down, he was not taking her job lightly, he simply was bringing a bit of humor into her life...there was such a difference now in her view of the world.

"Now, now," she teased, "someone has to carry on the real work of the world." With that, she kissed him once more, this time long and deep, then quickly rolled out of bed as his arms once again attempted to embrace her, hold her for himself.

"Well, what must be, must be, I suppose." He sighed, smiling as he lay sprawled over the wide bed, watching her every move. "Don't do that," he said suddenly as she reached for her long terry robe. She looked at him, puzzled.

"You look so lovely in the morning light. Don't cover up just yet," he asked, his voice reverent, his eyes never leaving her.

Faith blushed. No man she had dated had ever paid enough attention to her to offer such a compliment as Jim had just paid her. There were no words to express how grateful she was to him for bringing her back to the world of men and women, a world where femininity was to be prized above all and intelligence in a woman was to be respected. It was amazing that someone like Jim Stanten should be the man to teach her how to love again. Dropping the robe, she walked toward the bed and knelt on the floor, taking his head in her hands and kissing first his eyes and then his mouth.

"Thank you," she whispered. "You are such a dear, dear man and I love you very much." How sad there were no other words to express such a deep feeling, she thought to herself as she looked into his eyes.

"That better be the truth, lady," he said, returning the kisses in kind, "because I think we are going to have an absolutely wonderful time together for the rest of our lives."

Faith felt her heart leap to her throat. She knew he would be cautious and follow her lead. Faith understood his concern. After all she had been quite a changeable lady lately. She was grateful that he was being so gentle with her. The intentions of his last words were clear to her, and she was grateful he had not come right out and talked about marriage. Neither of them was ready to voice a deep commitment just yet. But, she knew she would not run anymore and she was sure he, too, understood her feelings.

"Now it's time for me to get ready for work. It's my last easy day before we start." She hesitated, hating even to think about what lay ahead. "Before we start the trial on Monday." There, she had said it. Strangely enough no feeling of depression overcame her, no harbinger of dread. Somehow she felt that no matter what the outcome of the trial, she and Jim would survive.

Skipping away from him and into the bathroom, she showered quickly and blew her hair dry in a matter of minutes. Peeking out into the bedroom she saw him, still lying in bed, gazing happily at the ceiling, his arms bent behind his head. He looked beautiful in there.

"How can you stand all this noise in the morning?" he asked loudly as she put the finishing touches on her make-up.

"What are you talking about? What noise?" she said, taking the opportunity to poke her head through the door once more, drinking in the beauty of his presence in her house.

"All those roller skaters and dogs and kids..." he answered her, twisting his head so that he could watch her in the bathroom mirror.

Faith fairly flew out of the bathroom at his words. Kids! How could she have forgotten to tell him the most important news of all. Well, maybe not more important than the evening they had spent together, their declaration of love, but nonetheless intricately tied with him.

"Jim, I forgot to tell you the reason I came to your place yesterday afternoon," she said breathlessly as she hurried about the room, knowing that the time was slipping away. "You'll never believe what I've decided to do."

"Yes, I will," he said, his voice low and throaty as he obviously enjoyed the scene playing out before him. Faith was a vision of loveliness there in the filtered light as she slipped into fragile bits of lingerie, one at a time. Piece after piece adorned her svelte body, the palest yellow lace panties and matching bra, a white-trimmed garter belt of lemon yellow and taupe-colored stockings. She had slipped her dainty feet into a pair of eggshell-colored pumps, which lenthened her shapely legs. Jim appeared so enthralled by her ritual that he had probably not heard what she was saying as she continued to jabber. But when she buttoned her beige silk blouse, he sat up in bed, all his senses now seemingly attuned to what she was saying.

"Say that again, Faith," he said cautiously.

"You nut," Faith said, playfully throwing a needle-point pillow at him, which he caught without much effort and held close to his chest. "Are you one of those people who don't wake up until eleven in the morning?"

"Just tell me what you were talking about; I didn't catch it all," he answered testily enough so that she raised her eyebrows and cast him a questioning glance. She was surprised by his terse tone but decided he simply wasn't a morning person.

"All right," she went on, "this time from the top.

I've decided to adopt Meg Cortland. After all, we're both alone for the most part, and I've always wanted to have children. Just think of everything I can do for her...."

"Faith," Jim broke into her happy speech, "that's crazy. What makes you think you can possibly care for a girl like Meg?" Faith stopped her dressing long enough to look at him deeply. She couldn't believe what he was saying. The liberal lawyer didn't think she could handle it.

"You don't think I could possibly care for a child?" she asked incredulously.

"Of course, you could. That's not what I meant and you know it. It's just that children like Meg are very special cases. Why not wait to have your own children? A child like that could be a handful of problems. Maybe not now, but when she gets older. Why, the kinds of things she's been through... you never know what kind of scars will be left, what sort of behavior will surface later."

"Well, look who's worried about scars on children. It was your client that put them there, you know," she answered, her anger causing her words to singe the air. How dare he pass judgment on her or Meg! Was this the same man who had held her in his arms a moment ago, gently declaring his love? She could hardly believe it with the way he was acting now.

"I know that. I understand. But it doesn't make me responsible for what happened to her. And because I'm the bad guy doesn't make you the avenging angel who has to make up for all my mistakes as well as those of my clients." His voice was rising to a fever pitch. Faith was amazed that he could possibly possess such emotions, but it still did not assuage her anger.

"I thought you'd be happy for me. After all, if you care that much, you would know that something like this would make me happy. I thought you wanted me to be happy," she challenged him with her words.

"I do, Faith, but you're not being reasonable," he shot back as she angrily zipped up her skirt and drew on her blazer.

"Reasonable! You're a fine one to talk about reason. You and that high and mighty life-style, you and your rationalization of your legal shenanigans. Just because I try to do something worthwhile, you always try to tear it down. You've done that since the first day I met you and I'm getting a little tired of it." Grabbing her briefcase she made to leave the room, but in an instant Jim was out of bed and beside her. His naked body shook with emotion as he took her by the shoulders, almost shaking her as he did so.

"I have never, ever, put down your work. I have made it very clear that I respect what you do. And, furthermore, it is unfair of you to continually bring my personal tastes into matters where they are of no concern. What we are talking about here," he said as his eyes burned into hers, "are lives. Two lives... yours and hers and maybe even mine. That would make three. What if you fail? What if you couldn't deal with what's to come in the future? It would kill you. Not only because you care about that girl but because you hate failure. You hate anything you can't control and understand. Face it... face yourself. Understand yourself before you make that kind of commitment!''

"I do," she fairly cried at him. "I understand that I need someone to care for, someone to love in my life. Is that so wrong? I want to share my life with that kid. I know I would be better for her than anyone else in this world. There is nothing wrong with that."

"Of course, there isn't," he answered, his voice softening as he fought to control his emotions, "but give it time. You've only seen her twice. You don't know what a relationship like that will entail in the long run. Stop making these snap decisions based on what your moral code is like. Don't play around with her life or yours." He was almost breathless from the tirade. Faith was confused, hurt that he did not share her enthusiasm over the idea of adopting Meg.

"I've got to go," she said petulantly, shaking herself loose from his grasp. Snatching her purse from her dressing table, she turned to leave the room, but he grabbed her arm, spinning her around to face him.

"Not yet, lady," he said determinedly.

"Let me go," Faith hissed back, hiding her desire to cling to him as she stood her ground.

"Not yet. Not until you tell me where I fit into this little plan of yours. Or hadn't you thought about that?" he asked, searching her face as though he could unlock her mind with his eyes.

"I just thought you'd be happy to hear about my plans, that's all," she said sulkily.

"That's not all. You know how I feel about you. You know that I wanted to see you again after the trial, that we were headed for something wonderful, something beautiful. Why would you want to ruin it? I thought you wanted me as much as I wanted you?''

"I do," she said, suddenly quiet. "I do want you" —her hand reached out and touched his face gently, persuasively as though that action could change his mind—"and I thought you would want Meg as much as I do. I thought you of all people would understand."

Please understand, she prayed silently to herself as he stood before her. At any other time, at any other moment, the sight of them would have reduced her to laughter. He, standing there naked as a baby; she, dressed as though she had just stepped out of a woman's magazine. But nothing was funny now. He was planting the seeds of doubt in her mind and she didn't want them to grow. All she wanted was Meg and Jim. She wanted them to be a family. Why couldn't he see that? Why did he have to be this way? She couldn't plead with him, her pride wouldn't let her.

"There hasn't been any time to even consider what we're going to do," he continued, hoping that now she was beginning to see reason. "How could you possibly expect me to fall instantly in love with the idea of a ready-made family? It's hard enough getting used to the idea that I love you. Do you know what kind of changes I'd be making if we decided to make this thing permanent, the freedom I'd be giving up and you would be, too? Don't you think we deserve a chance together first before we bring a third party into our relationship?"

"We've never discussed marriage," Faith shot back, anger covering her disappointment in his continued attempt at dissuasion. "I don't know what I expected. I suppose I did think that we might get that serious, but truly I haven't really thought about it in depth. But I have thought about Meg, and I do know that I want her and I'm going to have her. If you can't deal with it, with the idea that you helped make her the way she is, then maybe you can't deal with me."

With that she was gone. Her anger at him for being just like everyone else overriding the great sense of loss that was beginning to swirl about inside her mind and her body. She had tried to meet him half way. She had bent enough. It was his turn now and she was not going to give in. If it meant losing him, then so be it. So be it, she thought sadly as she pulled the cheery red Volkswagen out of the garage and sped off down the street toward the heart of Los Angeles.

# Chapter Nine

Faith had repaired her make-up in the parking lot before going up to the office. Unfortunately her efforts were sadly lacking and her face wore the look of a woman who had just been pierced to the core. No amount of rouge could hide her heartache. Throughout the morning Faith had sat behind her gigantic desk, her mind wandering, never stopping long enough on one thought to hold it, mull it over. She was exhausted to the point of being unable to lift a pencil or answer the phone.

Each time Darcy poked her head through the door to deliver a messsage, Faith found herself looking up hopefully, wondering if Jim had called, if he would call, to tell her the morning had all been a dreadful mistake. But, each time there was nothing. Judge Hardison's clerk had called to remind her of the nine o'clock court date on Monday. Mark MacMillan had called, and called again. But from Jim Stanten there was only silence. Finally as the noon hour approached and Faith's mood had still not lightened, Darcy confronted her.

"Faith, what is it? What's happened?" The black woman had cautiously approached her petite boss. "Didn't it go well with the little girl?"

Faith shrugged her shoulders noncommitally and continued to stare out the window. Moving into Faith's line of vision, Darcy stood her ground, hands on hips, silently demanding an answer. Faith only sighed once again, acting as though the large bulk of her secretary was no more than a cloud on a far horizon.

"Faith, stop it. You're scaring me half to death!" Darcy said sharply. There was a flicker in Faith's deep dark eyes, and she shook her head slightly, suddenly looking closely at Darcy, emerging from the depths of her deep depression.

"Darcy, I'm sorry. What were you saying?" Faith said, her voice sounding small and far away, the thin veil of sadness still about her eyes as though she were forcing herself to be attentive.

"That's better," Darcy said breathing a sigh of relief as she moved from the window and sat down heavily in one of the green chairs. She kept looking at Faith, making sure that the young woman's eyes still followed her.

"Now, what's going on? You've been sitting here like a zombie all morning. Even when you came in, you didn't say hello to Mr. Nardrom. There isn't anybody that doesn't return his greeting." Faith looked at her blankly.

"What are you talking about?" she asked, confused by what she had just heard. Mr. Nardrom, the U.S. Attorney of Los Angeles, had been gone for

weeks. She would have known if he were back. She
never would have committed such a professional faux
pas.

"Just what I said. The man himself was standing
right in front of you, grinning from ear to ear, and you
just waltzed by him like a little princess and locked
yourself in here. Now tell me what happened between
today and Wednesday to make you act like this."

Even though Darcy wasn't joking, Faith couldn't
help the smile that played about her lips. Somehow it
never rained but it poured...now Darcy was on her
case. Well she might as well spill the whole story,
otherwise she would never get any peace.

In fifteen minutes Darcy was privy to every word,
every action that had been spoken, had taken place, in
the last twenty-four hours, and now Faith sat back in
her chair feeling exhausted, not really caring what her
secretary's reaction would be. In a way she was almost
hoping that Darcy would leave without a word, leave
her to simply while away the day, watching the smog
roll by her open window. But Darcy had an opinion
about everything and this time was to be no exception. However the words were not tinged with her
usual good humor. Instead Darcy looked seriously at
the woman across the desk from her and thought
deeply before saying anything.

"Faith, honey," she started, pausing before she
went on as though she were trying to choose her
words carefully so as not to hurt or frighten the young
woman she had come to love and respect, "only you
know what you feel in your heart about either one of
those two people. Maybe you and Mr. Stanten were

never meant to be, but from the way you're hurting now, it seems highly unlikely." She waited for a moment as though she expected an answer, but Faith continued to stare out the window.

"You wouldn't be hurting the way you do now unless he had touched you so deeply that the imprint of his heart was on yours forever. I wouldn't write him off so fast. I wouldn't get rid of him just because he didn't agree with you about something so very important as that little girl." She took a deep, quick breath and continued before Faith could have said anything, even though the young woman did not look inclined to do so.

"Now that brings us to the girl. What you're talking about—adoption—why that's a big step. It takes some people years to decide whether to adopt a child, and then it's because the couple can't have any little ones of their own. But you're young and, well, Mr. Stanten probably loves you as much as you love him. If you wouldn't be so stubborn and give him a chance, there's a good possibility that things would work out and you could have your own babies, too." Faith looked up at Darcy, her face blank as she considered what the other woman was saying.

"But how do I really know what I feel about Jim?" Faith asked slowly, cautiously asking for the other woman's advice.

"Only you can answer that. Some women just know when a man is right for them. Some, like you, feel the need to analyze their relationship with a man, take it part piece by piece until only the ugly little parts are left instead of the whole beautiful person. That's dangerous, Faith. I'll hazard a guess that if you took yourself apart the same way you do him, you wouldn't like what you saw very much either."

"You're right, Darcy. I guess it's all those years of legal training. It makes me want to dig and dig until I understand everything completely. I don't want to make any mistakes, do you understand?" Faith asked, her eyes tearing into the other woman as though she could wrench an answer from her.

"Of course, I understand!" Darcy laughed, throwing her head back and studying the ceiling for a minute before looking directly at Faith. "Everyone feels that way. No one wants to feel the fool. But, honey, sometimes we just have to take the plunge." The words were kind with no sign of impatience.

"Oh, Darcy. I do love him. I really do and I would do anything for him. He makes me feel so wanted when we're together, so much like a woman. But I can't seem to stop thinking about him on a professional level when I'm away from him. Why do I continue to try to force him to be like me, to think like me?" Darcy looked at her young employer and saw the deep hurt and confusion in her. It was an ugly question but one that needed to be answered.

"Maybe it's because you're afraid if you don't change him, he may change you. If he did that, convinced you that there was some rhyme or reason to him, then that would negate everything you had worked for, clung to, all these years. Don't you think that maybe you need the reinforcement of his change. Maybe you're just not ready to accept anything less right now," Darcy said with a sigh, waiting for a moment before she continued so that her words would sink into Faith's mind. The petite, black-haired woman nodded, her eyes narrowing as she thought about Darcy's theory.

"But don't wait too long, Faith. You could kill any feeling he has for you by playing around with this one part of him. Is it worth exchanging his love for something like what he does for a living? Or for that of a child who might not be able to give you anything but heartache? I know sometimes you like to think of yourself alone against the world of crime. But before you're a criminal lawyer, you are a woman. Are you ready to push away a man who is ninety percent of what you want and ten percent of what you don't? Are you sure Meg is worth it?"

"I don't know if Meg is worth losing Jim over," Faith answered truthfully. "They seem to be two different subjects. I have no doubt that I was meant to take Meg. Certainly I feel sorry for her. But I feel so much more, as though some greater force is telling me to act now. I know I would be good for Meg. I'm not sure if I would be good for Jim or vice versa." Faith's hand moved to her forehead and she brushed back a nonexistent strand of hair, expressing the deep frustration she felt in that one gentle movement. "I guess I've got a lot of decisions to make," Faith said as she looked sheepishly at Darcy. The older woman noted how tired her young friend looked but said nothing. She simply nodded in agreement, sat for a minute longer, then quietly moved from her chair and left Faith to her thoughts.

Pros and cons of each situation swept across Faith's

mind. Somewhere in the distance Faith was aware of the sounds of secretaries and attorneys leaving for lunch. Typewriters shut down, doors opened and closed. Happy calls to friends faded into the hall.

For now she would not even consider Jim. She would try to live her life without him, without thinking of him until the trial was over. But Meg she could do something about. She was convinced that adopting her was the proper thing to do. Picking up the phone, she dialed Darcy's extension.

"I thought you might have gone to lunch," Faith began, attempting to sound as though their earlier conversation had never taken place.

"I thought you might need me," Darcy replied, her voice soft and caring and full of understanding.

"Just wanted you to know that I'm contacting Meg Cortland's case worker this afternoon." It was a statement. Faith had made up her mind.

"If that's what you want, then I'm proud to know you, Faith Karell." No words could have sounded better than Darcy's blessing and Faith smiled, beginning to relax for the first time that day. The hurt of Jim's words still lingered, as she knew they would, but the resolve to adopt Meg somehow eased that pain a tiny bit.

"Thanks," Faith replied, "that means a lot. Can you get me the number? I'd like to contact her right after the lunch hour."

"Faith," the secretary's voice called her back, "about Jim Stanten. Don't give up on him. Meg will make you happy but not the same way a man like him can."

"Thanks, but I'll just have to wait and see about that. But, I'm not sure he is the right man for me anymore."

"By whose rules? Yours are pretty hard to follow, you know."

"We'll just have to see, Darcy," Faith repeated and then hung up, feeling years older but none the wiser as she once again picked up the receiver and dialed the number of Meg's case worker.

Luckily the woman she had to speak to was still there and, after once again listening—politely this time—to the objections she raised regarding the adoption, Faith finally convinced her that she was determined in the matter. The case worker reluctantly promised to put the wheels in motion and hung up with a curt good-bye.

Faith almost slammed the phone down. Why were all these people trying to stand in her way? Everyday there were glowing reports of people who adopted kids, kids with handicaps, older kids. Certainly she knew the drawbacks but she wasn't one to give up a challenge. Faith knew she could handle whatever came along. Faith was beginning to feel as though Jim had called everyone in the city and told them to dissuade Faith from her quest. He was the first to know and he had rudely discouraged her. Now everyone else was doing the same. Didn't anybody care? Was she the only one willing to stand up and fight so that it would never happen to another child again?

Faith's ire was rising. Had she sat for a moment and truly examined her heart, she might have found a hidden recess where her stubborn nature was taking over. The more people tried to explain the pitfalls of such an arrangement, the more determined she was to carry out her plan.

Had she just taken that minute to clear her mind, Faith probably would have realized that lately she was giving no one a chance really to understand her. She was forcing herself, her convictions, on people who could make a difference in her life and expecting them to embrace her with open arms. If only she had taken the time to understand, to temper her actions, to wait for others to catch up with her enthusiasm, perhaps she would not hurt the way she did now. But Faith could not see what was happening to her; instead she was plunging headlong into her new life without heeding the warnings of people she admired and loved. To Faith, Meg was the answer to many desires and many problems. She was anxious to have the girl to herself, thrilled that she was to be a part of Meg's life, but not all her feelings were selfless.

There was, however, one objection that made sense to Faith. The welfare worker had advised against telling Meg of the adoption. After all, if for any reason the proceedings did not go as planned, Meg would be terribly disappointed. There was no way of telling how she might react. The only thing that really mattered was Meg's happiness and her mental well-being. They would have a whole lifetime together. It wouldn't kill Faith to keep her secret for a little while longer.

As she sat in her office, Faith tried to imagine Meg's reaction when she gave her the news. It was almost impossible to tell how the youngster would feel about it. After their day at the beach, Faith was sure that she would be happy, but she had to remember that the reaction might not be as ecstatic as one would expect. After all, Meg was still wary; she would wonder why she would now have one place to live. It would take a long time to hear the kind of childish laughter a girl of ten should be enjoying. But Faith even looked forward to that challenge.

*Oh Jim,* she thought suddenly, *if only it could have worked. It could have been so wonderful. Two of us would be planning now. Why couldn't it have been different?* Thoughts of Jim seemed to be inexorably linked with those of Meg. He had entwined himself in her life and, therefore, in the little girl's, yet seemed unaware of how much his presence had affected her. Faith continued to find it hard to believe that he had objected to the idea of adoption. Had she been so wrong about him? His sincerity seemed to encompass all things in life, but suddenly at the mention of Meg and Faith's plans for her, he had seemed to cut off all sense of caring. It was one area where he seemed to lack the sensitivity she had come to admire and love.

Well, what was done was done. Perhaps he would change his mind. He might even call her that very evening. But Faith would not allow her hopes to rise, knowing that he had the same strong sense of ethics and morality that she did, only it ran in a different direction. For all intents and purposes she was alone. There was no reason she couldn't make a home for Meg as a single mother; it was just sad that it had to be that way.

With a deep sigh Faith reached for her purse and stood up behind the desk. It was time to start again, time to pick up where she had left off before she met Jim Stanten. The old Faith was coming back to life, filled with determination. She had been self-sufficient before Jim; she could be so again. Faith knew she had to close the door on Jim and begin to recapture her quiet life. It had all been so simple then. What a shame, she allowed herself to think for an instant. Then she walked to the door and out of the office. Thank goodness she was blessed with a logical mind, Faith thought. She did not consider that she might be fooling herself, did not acknowledge the pain and loss that were very real. But it wasn't logic that was at play in her head, only the simple action of self-denial so that she would not feel, would not cry.

Once outside Faith breathed deeply, enjoying the feeling of being free of the confining office walls. Perching herself on the tall brick railings that flanked the wide courthouse staircase, Faith leaned back and watched the attorneys and clerks and agents race up and down. Everyone had somewhere to go except her. Just for today she wasn't going to rush. There was a weekend between now and Monday when she would have to begin the trial against Bennett, and she was going to make the most of it. Faith felt that she could spare another ten minutes just contemplating her next move.

She could go shopping and buy all those things she had been promising herelf lately. Her parents should be home, so she could stop and see them. But she quickly dismissed the thought. Today was for her. She would treat herself to the gift of time to gather her strength, have her hair done or get a facial.

"Miss Karell, so deep in thought on such a lovely day?" A cheery voice disturbed her before she could decide what she wanted to do. Looking down the stairs, she saw Judge Hardison with Mark MacMillan in tow, lumbering up the long flight of stone steps. She always enjoyed seeing him outside the courtroom. No one would ever believe he was a respected federal judge if one was to meet him on the street. The old man was given to strangely colored polyester suits, making him look more like a used car salesman than a legal wizard. Finally the two men stood before her, and Faith thought that Mark looked like a carbon copy of the judge.

"Not really deep in thought, Judge," Faith responded with a smile. "I'm just trying to decide what to do with the rest of the day. I'm going to play a little hookey." Her tone was conspiratorial and the judge picked up on the fun immediately.

"Oh, if I were only a few years younger and a few pounds lighter, I would join you. Can't think of anything more pleasant than following a pretty young woman all over the city when I'm supposed to be working." The old man nudged Mark, who smiled and nodded his hello to Faith.

Hardison's happy demeanor was contagious and Faith found herself smiling broadly at Mark. All thoughts of their differences seemed to wane there in the bright, warm sunlight. Mark was a nice man and a handsome one. Faith found herself forgiving him everything as the three of them made small talk. It was only the pressure of the impending trial that had made them all act a little oddly. Faith didn't know why she thought Mark should be any different than she was. After all she hadn't exactly been herself for a long time...chasing after Jim, making plans for everyone. Very unlike herself. So why shouldn't Mark have changed a little too? For an instant, though, Faith found herself comparing the two men, and Mark was coming out on the short end. Shaking her head, she dismissed the thoughts of Jim and turned her delicate face up to look into Judge Hardison's eyes, trying to pay attention to what he was saying.

"... we used to all go to the beach with a jug full of margaritas. It was a lot of fun." Faith smiled as though she had been listening to his tale intently. Unfortunately Mark had caught her lack of interest and was giving her a slightly reprimanding look.

"Judge," she said, "I can't imagine your being anything but the soul of propriety. How long has it been since you took a day off just because you felt like it?"

"Well, my dear, a very long time," he answered truthfully, "but don't tell anyone. I don't want to ruin my reputation as a playboy."

"I won't breathe a word," Faith answered. "Your secret's safe with me."

"So glad to hear that. Now since I can't accompany you on your escapades, what about my friend MacMillan here?" Hardison turned to look at Mark, planting a large red hand on the younger man's back and pushing him toward Faith. Before either of them had a chance to answer, the judge waved a hearty good-bye and left them alone.

Mark jumped up on the stone wall next to Faith and

rested his arms on his knees. His foot rhythmically
kicked the bricks as they sat in silence for a few moments. Each of them was unsure how to proceed, and
finally Mark spoke.

"Well," he said, lifting his head and looking up
into the smog-hazed sky, "what are you going to do
this afternoon?"

"Oh, I haven't quite decided yet," Faith replied,
still watching the people who were pouring in and out
of the federal building. "I might go and have my hair
done."

"I'd go with you, but the thought of waiting in a
beauty parlor isn't too appealing." The smile he bestowed on her was gorgeous and she returned it in
kind.

"Oh, that's okay. Actually I'm kind of looking forward to doing all kinds of girl things. I wouldn't wish
hours like that on any man." She laughed sweetly as
she said this and Mark sat up straighter beside her.

"It's nice to hear you laugh. You haven't done that
for a while," he said seriously. "Listen, Faith, I know
things have been kind of strained between us and I do
understand that we will never be more than friends. I
accept that now."

Faith looked at him closely. She really did appreciate
his declaration. Heaven knew she needed a friend.

"Thanks, Mark. I appreciate that and I would like
us to start again, too," she said softly and laid her
hand on his gently, a gesture that could only be con-
strued as sisterly. Sitting there with him in the sun,
Faith was almost sure that there would be no more
problems between them.

What did it really matter whether or not she ever knew the truth about the perjury claim? Maybe she was finally beginning to understand that she could only do so much for people, should only push them so far. She couldn't control Mark's actions or feelings any more than she could Jim's. And why should she want to? Didn't they have just as much right to their feelings and convictions as she did to hers?

Faith felt as though she was finally beginning to understand a few things. She asked too much of people. Live the way I want you to live was her motto. Now the sadness she felt for Mark was a healthy one. Faith could no more force him to tell her the truth than change Jim's feelings regarding her desire to adopt Meg. What really mattered now, she knew, was for her to live her life as a person and a professional, not everyone else's.

Squinting into the sun, they sat in silence until it almost became unbearable. She could feel Mark wanting her to tell him there could be more between them. But she couldn't. There was nothing more to do than let him get on with his day, with his life, too.

"Listen," she said, her happy smile a bit forced, "if I'm going to take full advantage of this afternoon, I better get going."

"Sure," he said, the disappointment evident on his face. "Faith," he ventured as she hopped down from the wall, "I, well, I just wanted to say if you ever need anything, I'm available."

"Thanks, Mark," she answered, squinting up at him. "I'll remember that."

As Faith turned and walked away, she knew that Mark understood she would not call.

Suddenly she felt freer than she thought possible. Her resolve to tackle life on her own terms was intact. She did not allow herself to think what would happen to that resolve when she met Jim Stanten in the court-room on Monday morning.

# Chapter Ten

Monday morning was gray at 6:00 A.M. when Faith Karell let herself into the cathedral-quiet federal building. She nodded her hello to the one guard who sat at a small table beside the bank of elevators, took the first open one she saw and entered into the complex that housed her office. Though there was not a soul to be found, Faith felt the building must be electrified.

Sparks of confidence seemed to fly from her as she reread her opening remarks and put the finishing touches on her questions, reacquainting herself with each and every fact that she already knew by heart. There was no feeling to compare with the one a trial lawyer experiences before entering a courtroom. Like a boxer sparring with a shadow before the title round, Faith went over and over her case in her mind. Facing the unseen opponent gave her a mental edge, allowing her to believe she had already won without the benefit of actual trial. It was a ploy that pumped the adrenaline to the boiling point, a ploy some used better than others, and Faith was a master. She was absolutely sure everything was in order. There was nothing she had missed during the long months of research and collaboration with the FBI. And the phone calls she had made to Meg over the last week had only reaffirmed her faith in the little girl. She would do all right on the stand.

For a moment she allowed her thoughts to wander back to the weekend. The last two days had flown by. Knowing she was going to be a mother soon, Faith had taken stock of all the things that had to be done. She had spent Saturday cleaning out the guest bedroom that she usually used as a study. This was to be Meg's room. Her daydreaming allowed her to decorate, erase the image and decorate again as she tried to decide what color would suit Meg best.

Sunday had been spent doing her usual Saturday chores. The washing had been interrupted by a call from her parents, and Faith had taken the opportunity to tell them about her plans. Her mother had been happy but restrained. Her father had voiced his objections but finally wished her luck.

Shaking her head to brush away the thoughts that threatened to disturb her concentration, she glanced at her watch, noting time was getting short. It was almost the moment when she would have to meet Jim on common ground. She shuddered involuntarily, the memories of him still bright and full in her mind as she wondered how she would handle herself. Like a professional was the only answer she could give. Faith knew that eventually the memories of him would fade so completely that she would be able to face him on the street or in the courtroom without a regret, without the tremor she was beginning to feel in the pit of her stomach. But today she would have to pretend that those feelings didn't exist and remember that she was ready for trial. Gathering up her files, she stuffed them into her briefcase and left the office and her personal concerns behind.

*Please, God,* she whispered to herself, *smile on us today.* Although she had never been overly religious, Faith thought the little prayer highly appropriate and felt sure that someone would be watching over her and Meg.

If Faith had been one given to fantasies, she would have thought her journey to the courtroom was perfect. For some reason the halls were nearly deserted and she could hear the slow and steady click of her heels reverberating through the building. It was as though she were Gary Cooper on his way to a showdown. *High Noon* would be the only appropriate title for the battle that was to come, if it hadn't been nine o'clock in the morning. She pushed the heavy doors aside and stood bathed in the soft, indirect lighting of the room, ready to drive the bad guys out of town. But the bad guys weren't unshaven banditos. They were beautifully dressed businessmen thoroughly entrenched in the year 1985, and one of them meant a lot to Faith Karell—personally and professionally.

Even though her first sighting of Jim was from the back of the court, Faith felt as though someone had just hit her in the stomach. Her breath left her, knocked out by the sight of the man with whom she had spent two nights of love. For an instant her eyes misted and then, controlling herself with an effort that was Sisyphean, she walked forward and entered the well, nodding to Jim coolly and ignoring Robert Bennett who characteristically pursed his lips and threw her a kiss.

Mark was already at the table, and Faith bid him a quiet good morning as she settled into her chair behind the prosecutor's table. At least she had made peace with the question of Mark and his integrity. There was no possibility that he could lie about anything during this trial, even if he wanted to. What was past was done as far as she was concerned. They could work together once again. Certainly things had changed, but there was no animosity, no burning desire for truth on her part.

"You're going on the stand first, then Wallace, then the distributor we've had under wraps. I'm going to put Meg on last. It will leave the biggest impression on the jury," Faith whispered to Mark, who nodded in reply.

"You sure Meg is going to hold up?" he asked quietly.

"I think so. It all depends on Jim—I mean Stanten. I have no idea what he's going to do on cross-examination. It could get really rough if he plays his hand—" Faith felt her heart sink. She knew Jim was too good an attorney not to give it his best, but she hoped that he would find some mercy in his heart for Meg, even if it was for Faith's sake. Hopefully he had that much respect for her. Looking over at the defense table, though, and noting the clean hard set of Jim's jaw, Faith could not imagine his doing anything less than his best, and she hated him for it. Hated him

for his professionalism as much as she loved him fo
the gentle man he was when he was with her and
court was behind them. My, but it hurt to look at him
think about him. Faith could feel her resolve melting
wishing he would look at her, smile at her, but he
remained impassive. Only his head moved now and
then toward his client as he listened to a whispered
word.

"How is Meg, anyway?" Mark asked, disturbing
her thoughts.

"Great...great," Faith stammered, once again
turning her attention to him. "She's come a long way
since I first met her. I don't think she really under-
stands what's going to happen in the next few days,"
Faith admitted, her concern evident. She wondered i
she should tell Mark about the adoption but decided
against it.

"It'll be all right," he said, trying to reassure her
Faith thought she detected a hint of sadness about
Mark and reached her hand under the long table to
give his a reassuring pat. As she withdrew her manicured fingers, the door of the judge's chamber opened
and Hardison entered the courtroom.

Behind them Faith could hear the curtailment of
the spectators' anxious whispering. The only sound
left in the courtroom was that of an artist whose pencil
was flying over her paper, capturing the images of the
judge, the lawyers and the defendant. Those drawings
would be flashed on every news channel for the next
week as the trial progressed, giving the proceedings a
romantic flavor, bringing notoriety to everyone involved. Only this time during the trial, Faith almost

wished her name wouldn't appear in the papers. This time, with the adoption proceedings now underway, she wanted commmplete anonymity, even though it was to be the milestone of her career.

Faith fought to bring her mind back to the proceedings at hand. Every nerve stood on end as she listened to the court clerk drone on with the opening remarks. A steely film seemed to cover her eyes as she dismissed all emotions from her mind, all longing from her body. With the determination of an Olympic athlete, Faith rose from her chair as Judge Hardison called upon her to begin her opening statement. It was always difficult not to make a plea at this point for the jury's understanding, but as always, she would stick to the facts, explaining carefully what the prosecution intended to prove.

As she approached the podium from which she must conduct all business, Faith went through her ritual that almost always went unnoticed by others. It was to her what a deep breath was to an actor. Carefully she put her notes on the high desk, straightened her shoulders and reached down to unbutton her jacket. Even though she could feel Jim's eyes boring into her back, she was ready.

"Good morning. My name is Faith Karell for the prosecution." she addressed the jury, her tone indicating her deep level of commitment. She knew that Jim would appear relaxed and confident; her only edge was that there was never any doubt in the jury's mind as to where she stood. She wanted them to know that this was not just a job, this was her calling.

"Today," she continued, looking at each of the jurors in turn, trying to read each's initial thoughts, "the government intends to prove beyond a shadow of a doubt that the accused Robert Bennett did with forethought and malice break the laws of the country and all the moral laws of the human race by exploiting children of all ages for his own financial gain.

"We intend to prove that Mr. Bennett has used these children in the most despicable manner possible by exploiting their sexuality and damaging their minds and bodies in the process in order to make prurient and pornographic films for export. Not only has Mr. Bennett been involved with this type of activity for the last year, but he has been involved in similar activities for the last ten years. With your permission we will prove these charges by using both the spirit and the letter of the law, and we ask your indulgence as we explore every avenue of Mr. Bennett's illegal activities. Thank you."

Faith buttoned her jacket, gathered her papers and turned back to her seat. The familiar tremor of nerves went through her as she crossed her legs and sat back in the chair. It would take a full day for her to get over her stage fright, but the feeling was an easy one to accept. It meant that her heart and soul were in her presentation. Now Jim rose from his seat and walked to the podium. Faith held her breath. His opening remarks would be telling and, no matter how it hurt to look at him, she knew she would have to watch his every move and be ready to counter his statements at any moment.

"Good morning, my name is Jim Stanten." He smiled warmly, letting the effect of his good looks and winning manner sink in. It was as though he were taking them all into his confidence with those few words, as though they were just sitting down to have a warming glass of wine. Oh, how she wished she had that kind of power, that kind of finesse.

"Today we are going to embark on an exploration to determine the right and wrong of a situation. Miss Karell has already told you about the wrong she thinks exists." Faith blushed at the mention of her name, as if those words were actually declarations of love. Damn, he could still do it to her even though her mind told her she should forget him.

"The defense intends to disprove all of the allegations against Mr. Bennett. We can show, beyond a shadow of a doubt, that the so-called evidence against him has been contrived and that the witnesses against him are unreliable. We further intend to show that since Mr. Bennett came to Los Angeles he has been gainfully involved in an import—export business that did not include the shipment of pornographic materials of any kind, especially those involving children. Thank you for your patience." He resumed his seat as though he were just going to check on something in the kitchen. There was no telltale signs of nervousness, and he simply sat back casually, but not too casually.

Faith looked at the jury. A few of the women had smiled at him as he left the podium, and one of the men was nodding, unconscious of the movement—a dangerous sign for Faith. Obviously the jury was quite disposed to believe Jim and had taken these few simple statements to heart. What a shame these people could be read so easily, Faith thought to herself. It would be a simple task to keep track of the proceedings from here on out.

A moment later Judge Hardison gave Faith permission to begin the case for the prosecution, and they were off and running. Mark had taken the stand and told in detail, as Faith questioned him, of the events leading up to the raid. Everything went smoothly for the rest of the day. Mark was relaxed and exuded the proper amount of animation, concern and professionalism. His testimony continued until the next day, and both she and Mark left the courtroom feeling drained.

Tuesday and Wednesday flew by. Faith felt reasonably sure that the jury was listening intently as she laid her case before them. Bennett had begun to show the strain of the three days of prosecution testimony and leaned closer to Jim on a more regular basis to confer with him as more and more damaging evidence was brought to light. Even Jim seemed to be feeling the effects of Faith's pointed questioning and the answers given by each successive witness. Agents and government-protected witnesses took the stand one after another, and Faith felt her strength growing each day. Jim's objections were overruled again and again. For each objection voiced, Faith could quote case after case that allowed the testimony to stand, and Jim began to take notes at a faster pace as she gracefully led her witnesses and the jury down the path to justice. She felt sure that now it was Jim who went home at night to his law books; his face looked strained and his eyes tired.

Even after three days, though, they had not spoken. Faith still wondered what he was feeling as they sat there in the courtroom so close to each other. He would smile and nod noncommittally each morning and then turn his attention to his client as Faith conferred with Mark. Unfortunately Faith was still unable to control her feelings of attraction each time she looked his way. It was only through the greatest discipline that she allowed herself to walk away each evening after the day was done without a word to him. How she still longed for his touch, wanted his arms about her still. If only he would give her some sign that despite their differences he still had some feeling for her.

She was becoming soft. How could she still want him while she saw him sitting with Bennett day after day, talking and laughing as though they were the best of friends? She must never forget that when it came time for the defense to present its case he would be relentless. He would not consider her a woman he had cared for. She was as much the enemy as he was and she must never forget.

Faith realized how easy it would be to deny the danger. She had held the floor for three glorious days, almost forgetting that Jim would also have a chance at her witnesses. The adrenaline flowing through her body tended to give her a feeling of euphoria. She knew instinctively that that feeling would begin to wane as each of her witnesses were torn down and tricked into saying things that they didn't mean. She had no doubt that Jim was an expert at this. Now, though, it didn't matter. The jury, the judge, all were hers. Tomorrow she would wrap up her case by putting Meg Cortland on the stand. For now she, Faith Karell, was the star.

Faith thoroughly enjoyed the warm and soothing bath that she sought upon returning home Wednesday night. She had pampered herself with a facial and a long soak, hoping to bring out all the tension she had known was building up inside her, even though she couldn't yet feel its physical effects. Finally relinquishing her watery bed and wrapping herself from head to foot in warm towels, she sat down by the phone and dialed Cornelia Jackson. Their conversation was short and served to ease Faith's mind regarding Meg's testimony the next day. The little girl seemed ready to testify and Faith hung up reassured. Although it wasn't late, Faith decided to take to her bed, watch the news and try to get to sleep early. She would have to be in top form for the next day's proceedings.

Switching on the TV, she climbed into her big bed and pulled the covers over her now-naked breasts. The sheets felt wonderful and Faith felt clean and alive. She snuggled down into the soft fabric of the bed and watched as the news passed before her eyes. Her eyes shut as the anchorwoman droned on and on, until she was disturbed by the announcement of a familiar name—her own.

Faith's eyes popped open, and there, on the screen, were the drawings the court artist had been making since the first day of the trial. Faith hardly listened to the commentary as she looked first at the drawing of herself, then that of Jim.

The woman artist had obviously spent a lot more

time considering his features, and she had captured his boyish charm. Sinking ever deeper into the pillows, Faith reached for the remote control by her bedside and flipped off the set. *When will this thing be over?* she almost moaned to herself. *I can't stand anymore. I don't want to see his face anymore.* She wanted to forget him but everywhere, everyday, he was there. If not him, then things to remind her of him and what he meant to her. If only she could be a robot, an unfeeling, unemotional piece of machinery. If only she could make herself that way. But then, what would be left for Meg? If she could turn her feelings off so readily, what kind of life could she make for the little girl who had to be taught about love? Over and over again she thought about Meg and Jim, Jim and Meg, until blissfully sleep overtook her and she enjoyed a long, deep, forgetful sleep. Waking the next morning, she felt refreshed, amazingly so, ready to guide Meg through the most difficult day of her life.

Cornelia Jackson sat directly behind Faith and Mark in the courtroom. As Faith had Meg called to the witness stand, she turned and looked at the older woman. Mrs. Jackson's face betrayed nothing. Only her eyes seemed to speak of all the concern pent up in both women. Meg, however, showed no emotion as she walked through the little swinging door that Faith held open for her. Her little sandy head was still bent as she walked, hand in hand with Faith, to the witness box. As Faith settled her in the big chair, she leaned close and whispered.

"You okay, honey?" she said, staring into the little girl's eyes and smiling broadly at her.

Meg nodded briskly and then whispered back, "I have my new dress on."

"I know, darling; you look beautiful," Faith answered, proud that she had brought such joy to Meg with the gift. *Just wait,* she thought, *just wait, Meg Cortland. I'll give you so much more than a dress.*

"Miss Karell, may we get on with this?" Judge Hardison broke in on them and Faith turned toward him momentarily.

"Certainly, Your Honor," she said apologetically, then returned to her place at the podium. Stealing a look at the jury, she noted that many of them were leaning forward with interest, looking at the girl who sat primly on the stand. A good sign. Faith addressed the judge.

"Your Honor," she said quietly, a hint of drama in her voice, "may I impress upon the court the necessity to treat this witness with the utmost understanding and gentleness." That was enough, Faith thought. Nothing flowery, just let them know that this girl is special.

"Your comments are noted and understood. You may proceed." It was clear even Hardison was effected by Meg's presence, but he remained cool as he sat on the bench. Faith wished she could see Jim's face during the examination but, that being impossible, she forged ahead.

"Meg," Faith said softly.

"Yes," the girl answered without any sign of fear.

"Meg, do you see anyone in this courtroom that you know who at one time did you harm?" Faith went in with her heavy guns immediately. The jury knew what the trial was about. They didn't have to go through the long and involved questioning that would take them through the events leading up to Meg's experience.

"Yes. That man," she answered, pointing directly at Robert Bennett, who, Faith saw, was beginning to perspire on his beautifully tailored shirt collar.

"Meg, I see that you are pointing to Mr. Bennett." The little girl nodded and Faith continued. "Can you tell me why you pointed him out? Where was it that you saw him?" Without hesitation Meg told the jury that she had seen him at three different hotels. The wonderful youngster even remembered the names of two of them. It was obvious that the jury was impressed, but so far Faith did not see the reaction she was looking for—that catch in the throat, the tear in the eye—but it would come.

"Thank you, Meg. You're doing very well." Faith had abandoned the usual curt voice she used during questioning for a more gentle tone, hoping not only to keep Meg calm but also to lull the jury into a mood of sympathy.

"Now, Meg," Faith began carefully, "I want you to tell us exactly what you did when you were at these hotels and exactly who told you to do it, all right?"

This was it. The clincher that would seal Bennett's fate. But Meg did not answer immediately. Her head fell to her chest as she contemplated her folded hands. Faith began to panic; she had seen this posture too many times not to know what it meant. Meg wasn't going to make it. She searched her mind for a way to bring the little girl out of herself, but before she could decide on which tactic to take, Meg's head shot up and her eyes glistened as she looked directly at Faith and began to speak.

For fifteen minutes Meg talked, her voice hollow, almost unearthly, as she recounted in dreadful detail the ordeals she had been through. One could have heard a pin drop in the courtroom. Even Robert Bennett seemed mesmerized by the story. The jury, down to the last man and woman, were moved to distraction by the tale. When it was over, even Faith found it difficult to speak. Finally Judge Hardison whispered that Meg was excused and the girl left the chair and ran to Faith's arms. Never bending, Faith simply put her arm around Meg, looked directly at the jury and pronounced three words that she knew would complete the powerful story.

"The prosecution rests." Her show was over and she led Meg back to Cornelia Jackson, who gathered the lavender-and-white bundle onto her lap to comfort her.

"Your Honor." Jim Stanten's voice cut through the emotionally charged air and startled almost everyone. It was as though the flood gates had been opened and everyone was dashed with freezing water. Each face in the jury box registered something different . . . anger, surprise, embarrassment. Yet Jim's ploy had worked beautifully. Now all eyes were on him. He had not allowed them time enough to wallow in their own emotions. He had jumped right in and given them something else to think about . . . him.

Faith's anger rose as he announced he would like to cross-examine the prosecution witnesses, beginning with Meg. My, but he was a shrewd one. The most damning testimony against Bennett and he was not going to let it lie for even an instant. He would attempt to disqualify everything Meg had said immediately so that in the next few days as he presented his own witnesses, it would be forgotten. Oh, he was smart not to bring her back toward the end of the trial! He was ruthless and Faith felt a stab of pain that was beginning to become a permanent part of her life tear at her heart once more. How could she still allow him to cause her pain?

"I see, Mr. Stanten." The judge was obviously displeased by this tactic but powerless to stop it. "How long will your cross-examination take?"

"It shouldn't be more than fifteen minutes, Your Honor," he said pleasantly but with enough subtlety to communicate a type of concern.

The judge looked at his watch. It was only eleven, far too early to call a lunch recess. With a sigh of resignation, Hardison nodded his approval, and Meg was once again brought up to the stand. Faith was amazed at how courageous Meg was.

Even though Jim was required to stand behind the podium while he questioned Meg, he seemed somehow to give the feeling that he and the little witness were very close. Leaning into, almost over, the podium, his personal warmth emanated toward Meg. She smiled at him weakly, unsure of what he was going to say to her. Her eyes were wide, her face calm, and she looked at him with trust, the same trust she had shown Faith.

"Good morning, Meg," Jim said sweetly.

"Good morning," Meg responded as she looked from the man with the glasses to Faith. Faith made a small sign to the girl and Meg smiled, sure that if Faith indicated everything was all right then it was.

"You told us quite a story this morning, didn't you?" he asked her softly.

"Yes sir." Her statement was pathetically simple. It wouldn't take much for Jim to reduce her to confusion. Dear *God*, Faith prayed as she watched, *let this be quick*.

"Do you remember exactly what happened to you in those rooms?" Jim went on.

"Yes. Just like I told it."

"Meg, then, could you tell us who was the first one to bring you to the hotel? Was it your foster mother, your foster father, or was it someone else? Now think hard, young lady." His voice was becoming stronger and Faith was getting nervous. The tone he was using would frighten anyone, much less the questions he was posing.

"I think it was my foster mother. She—" He cut her off before she had a chance to finish.

"You think, Meg? Aren't you sure of who took you to the hotel the first time?" The hard edge Faith had heard before crept into his voice so subtly that she wasn't even sure the jury was aware of it. Everyone's attention was focused on Meg, not on Jim, at this point.

"I'm sure it was my foster mother. I'm almost sure," she answered weakly.

"Now, Meg," he shot back, "when was the first

time you ever saw Mr. Bennett, the man you say did terrible things to you?''

''I don't know when. It was a long time after....'' Meg's head was beginning to bob. Her chin fell to rest on her chest and she raised her eyes to look at Faith for help. Faith could hardly contain herself and felt her anger rising to a feverish pitch as she watched the girl's agony.

''You say you don't know when you first saw him? That seems strange considering what you say he did, doesn't it, Meg?'' The little girl now sat silently, her slight body seeming to shrink away from the wooden box in which she sat.

''I don't know...'' she started, then hesitated. She seemed to be fighting with herself, struggling to get the words to come out of her mouth. ''I just know...I just know.''

Please, Meg, Faith thought, hoping her mind could somehow link with hers, please answer the question right.

''I just know he was the man who made me do it the first...the first time.'' She was stuttering and the catch in her throat was making her words almost unintelligible.

''Meg....'' Jim once again captured her attention. But, just as Faith was rising from her chair prepared to object to his line of questioning, angered that he would dare badger the fragile child, Jim spoke once more, cutting off any objection she might offer.

''No further questions, Your Honor.'' With that he turned back to his seat and settled himself behind the

defense table, ignoring Bennett's angry whispers and
staring straight ahead at the judge. Faith sank back
into her seat, her mouth open, the look of surprise on
her face evident to everyone in the courtroom.

"My God!" Mark whistled beside her. "What got
into him?"

Faith could not believe it. Jim Stanten had backed
down in the face of the little girl's testimony. What
had made him do it? He could have destroyed everything Faith and Meg had brought to the trial. He had
just thrown away the best chance he would have to
tear down the prosecution's case, and he didn't even
look worried. On the contrary, Jim Stanten looked as
though he had just experienced some sort of revela-
tion. There was a serene calm about him as he stared
into space.

Could it be that he had backed down for her? Faith
wondered. Impossible... or was it? He looked neither
left nor right and, at the end of the day, Bennett almost dragged him out of the courtroom, his two
goons hot in pursuit. As she watched them go, Faith
prayed that Jim would come to no harm. Even Bennett had to know that he had thrown away the chance
of a lifetime. He was no fool and he wasn't a gentleman either.

Faith had finally bundled Meg and Mrs. Jackson off
for the long ride to Long Beach and returned to her
office for a moment before heading home. Jim had
called only one witness after the lunch break, but the
testimony had been long and damaging.

It was a beautiful evening by the time she had
parked the car and had her dinner. The stars were

bright, the air warm and a soft breeze was coming off the quiet ocean. Faith was drawn toward the water's edge. For hours she sat on the cool sand, the gentle swells lapping at her feet as she tried to make some sense of what had happened that day. But no matter how long she thought, she could not pin down an answer concerning Jim's behavior. Perhaps she should call him, confront him with the strange turn of events. It could be that he was planning something, something that she was not aware of. A surprise witness, a case with greater strength than she already knew about. All of those things could account for his dismissing Meg so abruptly, just when he was ready to tear her to pieces.

There was something else, though. Something that Faith couldn't quite put her finger on. Was it a look, a gesture, a phrase that he had uttered that was bothering her? Was there a glimmer of recognition of the kind of havoc he could play with the little girl's life if he had continued? If that was it, then why hadn't he somehow signaled her, let her know that he had had a change of heart? Why let her go on wondering? Then suddenly she decided to speculate no longer. Faith was going to find out what had made him change.

Rising and dusting the sand from her slim jeans, Faith fairly ran back to her house. Breathlessly she picked up the phone and dialed directory assistance. Moving her lips she dialed again, attempting to remember the number she had been given without writing it down. The phone rang and rang again. Then just as she was about ready to give up, the receiver was lifted in the apartment in Westwood and Jim Stanten's cool, modulated voice spoke a word of greeting, inviting her to speak.

Her heart beat faster. It was the first time in over a week he had spoken directly to her, even though he was not aware it was she on the other end of the line. Once again he repeated his hello and she placed her hand over the receiver so he could not hear her nervous breathing. She couldn't do it. She couldn't speak to him now. Her pride would not let her. Her damn pride.

Quickly she hung up and leaned against the wall. If it had been some kind of sympathetic gesture for her in the courtroom, he would have called her. She couldn't be the first one to run back; she wouldn't be the first one to give in even if she never knew what had made him change his mind. Maybe someday she could tell him how grateful she was for what he did, but not now, not yet. Faith Karell's pride would not let her bend that night.

# Chapter Eleven

The defense's case dragged on. Witness after witness took the stand to testify in Robert Bennett's behalf. Next to the stream of people whom Jim called to the witness stand, Faith's case looked almost short-sighted. But she knew she had used everything in her arsenal, and even though there had been only a few people to speak out, she knew that each of them had been credible and that Meg's testimony still lingered on in the minds of the jury.

With each of Jim's witnesses, Faith watched the faces of the people in the jury box carefully. Every once in a while one of the jurors would nod in agreement or frown or even smile when Jim made a casually witty remark. Unfortunately she could not ready the twelve people as a body. There was now no way of telling what the final outcome of the trial would be.

By the time Faith rose to cross-examine Jim's witnesses, she was exhausted from the long hours of waiting, taking notes and conferring with Mark. But despite her weariness, her questioning was hard-hitting, professional, even brilliant at times. Never

once did the specter of Meg leave her mind as she
questioned everyone who took the stand. A few even
seemed to squirm as she fired her queries one after
another.

When the final day came—the day for the closing
statements—Faith felt drained but happy it was almost over. She knew that she had done the best she
could, the best that anyone could, and now it would
all be left in the hands of the reasonable men and
women of the jury. Only one cloud hung over her as
the trial drew to a close—Jim had still not spoken to
her. It was as though she could have been anyone, a
lowly prosecutor or the U.S. Attorney himself. He
treated her during the trial as though she were a non-
entity, a legal adversary and no more. He did not look
at her, made no move even to catch her eye, and it
hurt Faith and confused her more than she wanted to
admit. Still, though, there was something different
about him. Nothing anyone who did not know him
would point out. But Faith noticed. There was a slight
shading to his eyes, a soft trembling about his jaw as
he expertly guided himself and his witnesses through
the rest of the trial. The signs had been there ever
since he had cross-examined—or attemped to cross-
examine—Meg. Her heart went out to him even as
her mind continued to search for the reason he had
changed, even as her thoughts continued to condemn
him.

Now there was not time to consider Jim any longer.
The greatest challenge was about to be met—her clos-
ing statement. Jim had been brilliant, painting Robert
Bennett as a victim of an unrelenting and unjustified

attack by the U.S. Attorney's office, the FBI, and the IRS. Even Faith had begun to believe that the handsomely dressed man at the defense table could be guilty of nothing less than a minor traffic violation. She had been mesmerized along with everyone else by Jim's expert presentations of the facts as he wished them to be seen. Now it was her turn.

Gathering her last ounce of physical and mental strength, Faith rose, conscious that every movement she made had to make an impression on the jury and on Jim. She had pushed herself up from the table, her hands spread on the creamy dark surface of the wood, and stood there for only a moment as though she were contemplating the reflective surface.

Then Faith raised her shoulders and let her arms drop to her sides, raising her chin high as she did so. Turning toward the podium, she took four deliberate steps, turned, and faced the jury.

She let the courtroom silence surround her like a blanket. It was during this moment that Faith felt almost surreal. Between the time she reached the podium and the moment she began to speak, there was always an infusion of strength, a gift of courage that came from somewhere beyond the room. The strange thing was that no one else felt it. They knew something was happening to her, but they were never quite sure what was going on in that small moment of time.

Then her voice came out and filled the courtroom, building like a crescendo as she delivered her speech. The words were neither scathing nor vindictive, but filled with the emotion of true conviction.

"Meg Cortland," she began quietly, "was a victim

in the greatest sense of the word. The dictionary describes a victim as someone injured, destroyed or sacrificed under any of various conditions. Think about it... 'someone injured, destroyed or sacrificed.'" She let the three words sink into the juror's minds and looked at each of them with her wide dark eyes. "Can any of you think of any person, past or present, who fits that description better than Meg Cortland?"

"Injured," her voice rose a decibel, "yes, she was injured. Physically that little girl will never be the same, never know what it is like to make a choice in the matter of her own sexuality. Destroyed? Most definitely. Psychologically Meg will bear the scars of the treatment she experienced at the hands of Robert Bennett for the rest of her life. Sacrificed?" Her voice was now strong and confident as she continued. "Yes. But for what? Money, power, greed, enjoyment? All those things were the gods to whom Meg was sacrificed. Think now of the little girl you saw on the stand only a few short days ago and multiply that sad and wizened face by ten... no, twenty or perhaps a hundred other faces like hers. Then you see the full impact of what Robert Bennett and his kind are doing. The prosecution has shown you in detail not only the human suffering involved here but the highly professional actions of the FBI as they set about to determine the truth about Mr. Bennett.

"Our case is solid, backed up by not only the facts and figures of materials found on Mr. Bennett's premises and the testimony of his own employees, but backed up by the reality of what he has done to human lives and one human life in particular. Ladies and gentlemen of the jury, I can only ask you now to consider the stories laid before you during these past few days and then to think once more of the little girl who begs you to do what she cannot do herself—" Faith's voice faltered, the tremor of tears evident. "I beg you, along with Meg Cortland, to bring Robert Bennett to justice. Thank you."

When Faith finally reclaimed her seat next to Mark, she was aware that her face was wet with perspiration. She reached up and drew her hand softly over her damp cheek, then brushed her full hair back from her face. She dared not look in Jim's direction, fearing that if by any chance he caught her eye she might completely break down. The sadness of her own words was almost overwhelming as she thought about Meg. But there was another implication to her speech: Hadn't she and Jim also been victims in this whole mess? Weren't they too injured, destroyed, and sacrificed in the process? She had hurt him, he her. She had sacrificed for her beliefs just as he had. They had both destroyed their relationship because they could not give in and understand each other's deepest needs. Neither one could be the first to admit the wrongs they had committed against each other. Oh, Jim, how terribly sad, she thought as the judge quietly instructed the jury and dismissed them from the courtroom. It was 11:00 A.M.

"Faith." She felt a slight tug on her arm and turned to find Mark leaning toward her. "Everyone is gone."

Looking about her, she realized he was right. The entire courtroom had been cleared and she was still standing behind the table. She could not even remember rising in respect as the judge made his way to chambers. Jim was gone, Bennett no longer in sight. They were alone.

"Would you like to get some lunch while we wait?" Mark asked. "It might be a while before they come back with an answer."

Faith shook her head. "No thanks. I think I'll wait in my office." Mark nodded. He had seen her go through too many of these trials, seen her anxiety rise as each moment passed when the jury was in deliberation. It was better that she be alone.

"Okay," he said gently. "You go on up and I'll call you when they're about to come back. Just remember it may not even be today, so don't get your hopes up."

"Thanks, Mark," Faith said sincerely as she patted his hand. "You know you really did a fine job."

"I appreciate that, Faith," he answered almost shyly and she wondered if he still carried a torch for her. But she was too tired to consider the possibility as she made her way back to the office. Darcy had a steaming cup of tea waiting on her desk when she walked in and, as usual, did not attempt to make conversation as Faith dragged herself down the hall and closed the door to her office.

Five hours later Darcy heard the phone ring in Faith's office. The door opened a moment later and Faith rushed out the door. The jury was in. It took only a few minutes for her to arrive in the courtroom and then take her place behind the long table, her breath coming in short, labored spurts. The jurors were just coming through the door, the judge waiting to approach the bench. Jim and Bennett were standing straight and tall, neither looking terribly worried. Finally Judge Hardison settled himself in his tall chair and turned to the jury.

"Mr. Foreman, have you reached a verdict?" he commanded. The handsome, middle-aged man, Mr. Christoph, rose from his seat and addressed the black-robed judge.

"We have, Your Honor," the man began, his voice cracking from embarrassment at having to speak before so many people. "We find the defendant, Robert Bennett, guilty on the count of distributing prurient and pornographic materials both in the United States and abroad."

"How do you find on the count of aggravated assault against Meg Cortland?" the judge queried. Faith closed her eyes and held her breath. Half the battle was won; there was no way they could lose the other half.

"We find the defendant—" the man hesitated, wiped his brow and glanced at Faith. She felt her heart stop. It was not a good sign. She willed the man to continue. "We find him not guilty, holding to a reasonable doubt of his participation."

Faith thought she was going to faint. She must have heard the man wrong. They couldn't possibly know what they were doing. She wanted to scream, to lash out at all of them. How could they? How dare they? These reasonable men and women—how could they possibly know what they were saying?

"I see," Judge Hardison said almost to himself. Mr. Christoph sat down and looked steadfastly at the floor, as did most of the others. Faith looked up at the judge, her eyes pleading with him to sentence to the full extent, even overstep his bounds in this matter. She tried to make him see that it was all wrong. She was willing her mind into his, but she knew instinctively that, even if she could have shouted out her desire, he would do nothing more than what the law allowed.

"Mr. Robert Bennett," Hardison began, his voice halfhearted, "you are hereby charged with the crime of distributing pornographic materials and sentenced to three years in the federal penitentiary. No doubt your attorney will see fit to appeal this case. That is all." With that the judge rose and left the courtroom, an air of sadness following him through the hidden door.

Faith sunk into her chair and felt Mark's arm around her. At that moment she was more than grateful for his strength. It was all so ludicrous. Not only did the jury let him go, but the judge could only put him away for three years. He would be forced to serve only eighteen months unless Jim won the appeal. Then Bennett would never see the inside of a jail cell. Her world was reeling...she needed air...she had to get out of the courtroom.

Grabbing her purse, she pushed her way past the spectators and reporters, ignoring Jim and Bennett and Mark as she ran for her car, ran for the safety of her home.

For a long time Faith sat in the gathering dark. The house was silent. Tonight there would be no music, no celebratory call to Meg and Mrs. Jackson. How could she call them and tell them that she had let them down, that the system had let them down? There were simply no words to describe the hurt, the pain, she was feeling at that moment and would feel for months to come. Perhaps the thing that had hurt even more than the simplistic sentence was the fact that it had been Jim who had brought this upon her. He had played his cards right. He had gained the jury's affection by backing off with Meg and then bringing in his big guns. He was so slick. For once in his life he should have known it was wrong, should have cared enough not to do his best. If it had been she... if it had been she on the other side— No, she couldn't finish the sentence. Faith knew that had she been on the other side she would not have relented for one moment. More than likely she wouldn't even have left Meg alone. That was the mark of a good, no, a great attorney.

Finally she could stand it no longer. She couldn't sit in the little pink bungalow so close to the people who had played a part in her life for so long. She didn't want to be reminded of Jim or the trial or even of Meg. She had to get out and she knew exactly where to go.

The ride up to the family cabin in Lake Arrowhead was therapeutic. Throwing caution to the wind, Faith had sped through the night across the flat lands of Orange County and finally on up into the San Bernardino Mountains. Slowing only when the roads became slick with frost and snow, she was careful enough to pay attention to each winding curve as it came her way. Higher and higher she drove into the mountains, the hard driving commanding all her attention, until finally she pulled into a driveway almost hidden by the tall pine trees that flanked the cabin.

Stepping out of the car, she took a deep breath, the cold crisp air piercing her lungs, cleansing her of the smog and heat of the city far, far below her. California was indeed wonderful. The September heat in the city could be escaped by a short drive to the early-wintered mountains.

Gently prodding Bailiff who had slept on the seat beside her during the entire trip, she made her way to the front door, searched for the hidden key and let herself into the immense second home her family always kept ready for emergenciés such as this. It was their haven, and silently Faith blessed her father's success, which had allowed him such an extravagance. Completing only the necessary tasks of turning on the water and the heat, Faith succumbed to exhaustion and collapsed into one of the deep beds, sleeping as though she would never wake.

But wake she did after a long and refreshing respite. Faith rose and opened the rustic shutters, noting that the snow she had thought so heavy the night before was only a patchy covering on the ground. Even though the mountains were not a fairyland of white, there was still a glistening halo surrounding the trees and cabins. The Lake was like a giant shining disk. Everything was clean and wholesome, yet Faith could only appreciate what her eyes could see. The usual soul-thrilling excitement had been replaced by the deepest depression she had ever experienced. Perhaps a walk would do some good, clear her head, drive Jim and Meg out of her mind for a while.

Settling Bailiff with his breakfast, she donned a pair of clean jeans and a heavy sweater, closing the door solidly as she left the house. The air was biting as she walked among the pines, but neither that nor the exquisite scenery helped to revive her spirits. When she could walk no longer, she sat on a giant boulder and thought, only to find those thoughts created too much pain to be alone with. It was better to exhaust herself through the physical exercise of walking. Finally, laconically, she turned back toward the cabin. Faith had no idea what time it was nor did she care. She didn't have to be back at work for two whole days. Maybe in that time she would be able to reconcile herself to the facts of her existence, put herself back together and get ready for the next battle, the next trial.

She picked up a branch that lay at her feet and used it as a walking stick, digging it into the earth with such force that she thought it might break at any moment. If anyone would have seen her, they would have thought her crazy, but Faith could think of no other way to relieve herself of some of the anger that still lingered in her heart.

Lifting her head, she peered through the forest and noted that the house was just ahead. Suddenly her head snapped up and she strained to see through the trees. There was another car parked beside hers and a figure standing on the porch, arms wrapped around his body in an attempt to keep warm. Faith stopped and rubbed her eyes, dropping the stick as she did so. It was he!

"Faith," Jim hollered frantically, his voice reverberating through the quiet mountains. "Faith, I know you're in there. Now open this door!"

For the first time in days, Faith allowed herself to smile. He was always so sure he was right, Jim Stanten was. For once he was wrong. Quietly she walked up to the house, her hands shaking as she stuffed them in the pockets of her jeans. He had just begun to pound on the door.

"Are you looking for me?" she asked quietly, trying to keep her voice under control. He spun around to face her and Faith thought she would surely melt at the sight of his handsome face. They had not stood so closely for so long, and she had almost forgotten the devastating effect he had on her physically. She could feel the tremors begin in the pit of her stomach, traveling up to her heart. Her breath caught in her throat as his dancing eyes searched her face, and his smile faded when it was not returned.

"I thought you were inside," he said sheepishly, unsure of how to react to her sudden appearance, her seemingly harsh stance.

"I gather that," she answered, making no move to approach him. But her immobility was not out of anger, as he suspected, rather she forced herself to stand her ground so that she would not run to his arms, forget why they would never work together. The silence grew as they continued to search each other's eyes. There was really nothing to say to him, yet she wanted desperately to speak. Where could she begin? Then it struck her. The best place was with the obvious.

"How did you find me?" Her voice was still curt, but she knew that he could read her desire like a book. It would be difficult to hide her feelings if he stayed much longer.

"Darcy," he answered. "She knew about your hideaway. Then a call to your mother and, well, here I am."

"I see" was all she could think to say and once again there were no words between them. But Faith knew she had to continue the conversation as he started to move toward her. If he came any closer, she would melt into his arms, and that was the last thing she wanted to do, the last thing she knew she should do. Her mind flew in all directions as she relived the moments during the trial, the condemnation of her plans to adopt Meg. She must remember those things. She must not give in and lose herself to him, too.

"Would you like a cup of coffee before you go?" she asked, knowing that her tone was less than inviting.

"Sure." He nodded.

Faith moved up the old wooden steps toward the door, lowering her eyes as she passed him and put the key in the lock. It swung open easily and a rush of inviting warm air hit them as they entered. Faith turned and closed the door behind her, breathing deeply before she could face him. His voice filled the cabin as she heard him move into the center of the room.

"Hi, Bailiff, long time no see." Faith turned in time to see him sweep the cat into his arms, but he did not look up and meet her eyes.

"I'll get the coffee," Faith said going to the kitchen. While the coffee perked, she moved about getting cups and napkins, sugar and cream and arranging it all on a tray. Though it was more formal than her normal coffee break at the cabin, she knew she must do something to keep her mind off the man in the other room.

Finally, carrying the tray, she walked back to the living room. Jim still held Bailiff but now stood looking out of the large picture window.

"Here it is. Be careful, it's hot," she said, putting a cup on the edge of the table. But he made no move to take it, simply watched as she went about her chore, then turned back to look at the trees and mountains.

"It will be dark soon. The road was already slick when I drove up. I'm not used to mountain driving." His statement was conversational but underlying was his hope that he might stay with her, talk to her. Bailiff wiggled and jumped from his arms.

"Must run in the family," he said wryly as he watched the fleeing cat.

"That was uncalled for," Faith responded. She had left for a good reason. There was a difference. "But you are right. It will be getting dark. Perhaps you should start now and forget the coffee."

Jim's eyes darkened as Faith stood and watched him. Then in two swift steps he was beside her, wrenching the tray from her hands, the hot coffee from the remaining cup spilling on the small piece of ground between them as he put it on the old coffee table. Grabbing her shoulders, he spun her into him, crushing her to his body, which now shivered from desire rather than cold. His lips covered her face with frantic kisses.

Faith felt her resistance wane, and in a moment her arms were about him, welcoming his advances until her mind took over and she pushed him away from her, rushing to a distance of safety to be free of his overpoweringly sexual influence.

"What do you want from me?" She screamed at him, her voice filling with tears, her body racked with desire and shame for wanting him so. "Haven't you done enough already? Haven't you destroyed everything I worked for, everything I believe in? Haven't you destroyed my dreams of a family? Why do you torture me like this?" In an instant she was reduced to sobbing in front of him, shamed at her lack of control, trying to stand straight before him in order to regain some semblance of dignity but failing miserably.

He did not approach her, did not try to take her in his arms again. Instead, breathing deeply, he stood helplessly watching her pain, wrestling with his desire. His heart reached out to her even though he knew his arms could not. Finally, desperately wanting to help her, he spoke.

"Faith," he said gently, holding his ground, "I'm so sorry. I did what I had to just as you did. I'm sorry it turned out the way it did. And I've never been sorry for winning a trial in my entire career." He searched for the words that would ease her hurt and, finding none, simply forged ahead, hoping the sound of his voice might somehow comfort her, the news he had brought might calm her.

"Faith, I came to tell you," he went on as he watched her shoulders straighten, her sobbing abate, leaving only tracks of clear tears running down her cheeks, "I'm not handling the appeal. I've given up on the Bennett case."

Faith stared at him through watery red eyes, knowing that, if he were telling the truth, he must also be hurting. It would go against everything he was, not to play the hand out to the end.

Noting her incredulous look, he rushed ahead. "It's true. I'm leaving that to someone else. I couldn't hurt you or Meg any more than I already have. I couldn't let you know during the trial... neither of us needed the pressure. But I made up my mind when I saw her on the stand. I'm not an ogre, you know. You must know I couldn't possibly be that cruel. If you had never called her as a witness, I wouldn't be here now. But you did. A physician can't treat those close to him. I couldn't destroy either of you."

"You mean that wasn't planned? You didn't stop cross-examining her because you wanted sympathy?" Faith could hardly believe her ears.

"Heavens, Faith," Jim said, turning back toward the window for an instant and dragging his hand through his hair before he moved toward her, "how could you think that? I told you once before I enjoyed playing the game. I do like to use my skill, but there is a limit." He stood before her now, his voice carrying the edge of hurt, and Faith's heart went out to him as he raised his hands to take her by the shoulders, then thought better of it, and lowered them to his side.

"I can bend, Faith. I just hope you can." He was not pleading with her now. Jim Stanten was simply giving her an option, admitting she had a right to choose. But Faith could see what he wanted her answer to be. "I love you, Faith." He could think of no other words to defend himself. There were no other words that would convince her of his sincerity.

As he stood before her, his eyes searching her face for some sort of sign, Faith raised her delicate hand toward his face and ran her fingers down the side of his strong jaw gently. Slowly she moved into him, wrapping her arms around his neck, nuzzling her face into the warm crook of his shoulder.

Faith heard the deep sigh that emanated from within Jim as his chin caressed her soft hair and his arms hesitantly encircled her, pulling her ever closer to him. As they stood there, swaying in each other's arms, Faith was overwhelmed by the realization that he had put himself in professional jeopardy by refusing the appeal. She was ashamed of her harsh judgment of him at the trial.

"I know I've caused you many disappointments, Faith," he said quietly, his voice muffled by her cascading hair. "Perhaps I have no reason to hope now. But I have to tell you: I want you more than anything on this earth, if you'll have me." As his words faded into nothingness, Faith realized that she, too, had caused him pain. Why did she always manage to think only of herself? In the weeks since they had last been together, she had only considered her feelings and now her shame was evident.

"I love you, too, my darling," she whispered, stroking his hair. "I love you and I'm sorry. I've been so unfair."

"Does that mean we have a chance?" he asked,

moving his head so that he could look into her face, read the answers before he actually heard them. "I came here to tell you that I wasn't handling the appeal, hoping it would make you realize that I'm willing to meet you halfway.

"I don't want to fight you. I want to love you and care for you for the rest of your life, but I'm not going to be run over by the woman I love. I'm not going to let you run my life, nor will I try to run yours." The words seemed to be torn from him as though, if she demanded his change, he would do it even if complying meant the disintegration of his spirit.

"I want us to be friends and lovers. Accept each other for our faults and our strengths." His voice finally broke and tears began forming at the corners of his eyes as she gathered him close to her.

"What is it you want me to do?" she asked softly.

"Faith, I want time for us." He raised his head, his eyes dry now, but his voice still shaking. "The morning you told me about Meg I wasn't angry. I was hurt. It was as though you cared more for her than for me. Then, when I thought about it, I realized that I cared what happened to her, too, and that you were just excited about the prospect of adopting her. That was fine. But I want what's right for us first. Until we have that, until we have time together, we can never make a proper home for her. I guess I didn't realize how much I could care for her until she was on that stand. That day in your apartment I wanted her only because you did." Disentangling himself from her, he took her hand and led her to the rickety old sofa, gently lowered her onto the cushions and knelt beside her.

"My darling, there is no sin in compromising, bending a little. Give us a bit of time together. Think about Meg and me and everyone else's life you touch and realize that all our needs are different. Let's become the kind of parents Meg needs before we take her into our home. Please let me love you for just a minute all by ourselves, and I promise that you'll never regret your decision. Have faith in me."

Jim lowered his head onto her lap, silently resting his case, waiting for the verdict that would be spoken by a jury of one.

Instead of speaking, Faith reached down and cupped her hands about his smooth chin, raising his eyes to hers, searching the face of the man at her feet. Finally she saw him clearly. A man strong enough to bend, gentle enough to care, wise enough to understand her. Slowly she bent and covered his lips with hers, giving him the answer he sought, sealing their fate with her wordless judgment. There was no doubt that the defense had won.

# Get this book FREE!

## Mail to:
**Harlequin Reader Service**

In the U.S.
2504 West Southern Ave.
Tempe, AZ 85282

In Canada
P.O. Box 2800, Postal Station A
5170 Yonge St., Willowdale, Ont. M2N 6J3

**YES!** I want to be one of the first to discover **Harlequin American Romance.** Send me FREE and without obligation *Twice in a Lifetime.* If you do not hear from me after I have examined my FREE book, please send me the 4 new **Harlequin American Romances** each month as soon as they come off the presses. I understand that I will be billed only $2.25 for each book (total $9.00). There are no shipping or handling charges. There is no minimum number of books that I have to purchase. In fact, I may cancel this arrangement at any time. *Twice in a Lifetime* is mine to keep as a FREE gift, even if I do not buy any additional books.

154-BPA-NAZB

Name _____ (please print)

Address _____ Apt. no. _____

City _____ State/Prov. _____ Zip/Postal Code _____

Signature (If under 18, parent or guardian must sign.)

This offer is limited to one order per household and not valid to current Harlequin American Romance subscribers. We reserve the right to exercise discretion in granting membership. If price changes are necessary, you will be notified.

Offer expires May 31, 1985

AMR-SUB-2

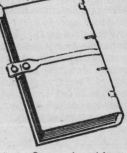